Brassy Women

by

Chris Vale

Dales Large Print Books
Long Preston, North Yorkshire,
BD23 4ND, England.

British Library Cataloguing in Publication Data.

Vale, Chris
    Brassy women.

    A catalogue record of this book is
    available from the British Library

    ISBN   978-1-84262-721-1 pbk

First published in Great Britain in 2009 by The Book Guild

Copyright © Chris Vale 2009

Cover illustration by arrangement with
The Book Guild Publishing

The right of Chris Vale to be identified as the author of this work
has been asserted in accordance with the Copyright, Designs
and Patents Act, 1988

Published in Large Print 2009 by arrangement with
The Book Guild Publishing

Dales Large Print is an imprint of Library Magna Books Ltd.

Printed and bound in Great Britain by
T.J. (International) Ltd., Cornwall, PL28 8RW

BRASSY WOMEN

These ladies are nothing if not brazen to the end!

Lancashire in the early 1960s. The heady world of the brass band is almost entirely a male preserve. Except for the Adlington Ladies. Put together in piecemeal fashion with conductor Lucy at the helm, their aim is to beat the all-male Great Hulme Motors Band at next year's brass band festival. Each member of the women's band has her own life outside band practice, and their trials and tribulations are related with gentle northern humour. Even their motley collection of instruments presents problems, with the chronic lack of a drum kit (and a drummer) ... and a piano that turns traitor!

The action takes place in the early sixties, when women brass players were few and not every family owned a car. All the characters are imaginary. No resemblance to any living person is intended.

Prologue

It was a chilly winter's evening towards the end of 1960. A crescent moon was swanning among a coterie of stars above the rooftops of a residential estate on the outskirts of Chorley. The northerly gale had swung round to somewhere south of east and dropped to a mere force two. So all was quiet. Then the chugging of an old engine announced the approach of a van, which coughed to a halt with its nearside wheels on a grass verge, leaving enough road for cars to pass. By the light of a nearby lamp post, the words *Bill Ainscough's Hot Stompers* could have been discerned on its sides, had anybody with discernment been about. But it was teatime. The residents were home from work but not yet gone out on any social activities.

The sisters had planned it carefully. This was the moment. The driver's door and the front passenger door opened in unison. Alice on one side and Gladys on the other jumped rather awkwardly out with one accord.

'Ouch!' squeaked Alice, who had landed on the pitted verge, 'I think I've ricked my ankle!'

'Not now, Alice, please,' snapped Gladys,

making her way to the back of the van and opening the double doors.

'I've got everything ready,' came Florence's voice from inside, rather too loudly, but Florence was always loud. She could not help it.

'So pass them out, then, will you?' Gladys asked her. 'Quietly, if you can.'

'Here – Mary, that's Gladys's.' Florence handed it to the fourth sister, who had been travelling in the back of the van with her. 'Careful, now.'

Mary handed it to the waiting Gladys.

'Where's Alice, then?'

'Oh she thinks she's hurt her ankle. She never could jump.'

'We can't do without her. She's first.'

'It's OK,' Alice limped up, 'I'll suffer. It's in a good cause.'

Another long object was passed from one to the other with all due care and attention from pair of hands to pair of hands until it nestled safely in Alice's. Florence and Mary climbed gingerly out of the back, being careful to spare their ankles, and the four of them stood looking around and getting their bearings before advancing to a central patch of grass. Somewhere a dog barked.

'Have you got the box?'

'No, you've got it.'

'I haven't got it.'

'It's all right,' Mary told them. 'I've got one.'

The dandelion patch they were standing on was surrounded by a circle of houses.

'Ready,' hissed Alice, 'after four.'

They put their trombones to their mouths (a euphonium in Mary's case) and piped up bravely with 'Hark! The Herald Angels Sing'.

The sound seemed to carry all the way to Wigan in the still air. More dogs barked. Of people there were none.

'Give them another verse,' Florrie ordered, wiping her nose. 'Give them two.'

They played two more verses and still no doors opened. A car drove in and pulled up about thirty yards away. The occupant got out, slammed his door and entered his house without so much as a wave.

'I knew it couldn't be that easy,' sighed Mary, unclipping her small book of euphonium carol parts from the lyre-shaped clip which held it, then turning the pages. 'What shall we give them next?'

'"Christians Awake", I reckon,' said Florence.

They took her at her word, found the page, and were just about to blow the first note when loud chimes rang rudely out and an ice-cream van swung round the corner.

'Ice cream? In this weather?'

'Would you believe it!'

'Let's go home,' pleaded Gladys. 'I'm frozen.'

'Wait!' whispered Alice. 'Look at that.'

People were emerging from doorways. Most of them were children, but several adults came with them, armed with their purses.

'Customers!'

The quartet edged closer to within a few yards of the queue and started to play. The children, once served, were drawn to the unusual sight and sound. They stood looking and licking, then wanting to be given coins to put in the box. By the time the spectators had all had enough and gone, a healthy start had been made to the sisters' collection.

The musicians went out again whenever they could all spare an evening. Some nights were better than others, but they always came back with something. They began to look further than estates and try some of the larger houses – the ones that had drives you could turn into and park. It was at one of these that they met Eddie Pickerskill.

He was an old man, but he stood on his step without a shiver and listened at length. After three carols he asked them to come in and have a glass of sherry. The sisters looked at one another. Well, there were four of them. Safety in numbers.

'Only four of you,' he remarked, pouring out the sherries with a shaking hand, 'and all lasses.'

'That's right,' said Mary politely.

'Our dad taught us to play,' added Florence, grasping the small glass with a large paw. She was used to Guinness.

'And no cornets,' he continued; 'but it doesn't matter. Sounds champion.'

'Thanks.'

'Our dad's Bill Ainscough,' Gladys told him, by way of explanation.

'Ah!' it registered. 'Well well well. So you're Bill's girls. I should have known. I saw you years ago playing with your dad. But you were only little then. Sit ye down. Have you got the time?'

They sat. The room was full of junk, but some of it was good junk.

'We're collecting for a van for the handicapped,' Mary told him. 'So that they can be taken for trips to the seaside and the zoo. Things like that.'

'I'll give you summat towards it.'

He reached in his pocket and brought out a wallet from which he extracted two five pound notes.

'That's ten pounds!' Mary told him in some concern.

'I know. I know. I've not gone demented yet.'

'Are you sure you want to give all that?'

He ignored the question.

'You play reet well,' he told them. 'And not just for lasses either. Proper well. Have you got any friends as plays like you – I mean

13

ladies, not blokes. Cornets and basses and whatnot?'

'You mean a whole band?'

'Aye. A whole band. Of ladies.'

They shook their heads. He was bitterly disappointed.

'Pity about that. More sherry?'

'No thanks,' Gladys came in quickly on behalf of them

He put the top back on his cut-glass decanter and sighed. 'I wish you could have found yourselves a whole band of lasses as plays like you do. You could have given us blokes something to think about I can tell you.'

'I don't think there's enough of us as plays,' Mary hazarded.

'Have you ever asked around? Checked to see, like?'

'Never thought of it,' said Gladys.

'Nobody's ever suggested it,' said Alice.

'Till now,' added Florence.

'What do you want a women's band for, anyway?'

'I tell you,' Eddie told them. 'If you and a band of lasses like yourselves could have gone in for t'Brass Festival and beaten the pants off Great Hulme Motors...' he raised his glass to them, '...I'd have bought you your van – straight off.'

He took a good mouthful of sherry. There was a startled silence.

14

'You wouldn't care to put that in writing, would you?'

That was Florence; the serious musician. Gladys gave her a painful dig with her elbow.

'Florence! Don't be rude! He doesn't mean it.'

'Who doesn't mean it?'

He opened his solid oak desk, took a piece of cheap, ready-lined paper and a biro and wrote that he, Edward James Pickerskill, hereby undertook to supply...

He raised his bushy white eyebrows at them as if to say 'supply who?'

Mary, with the money box, spoke up.

'Mary Rawlinson,' she prompted him.

'...supply Mary Rawlinson with one new van suitable for transporting the handicapped. This I would do in the event of a band containing the four ladies present and completely composed of female persons succeeding in obtaining more marks than Great Hulme Motors Band at the next South Lancashire Festival of Brass,' he saw their jaws drop, 'or the one after. Anything else?'

'N-no. That will do nicely, thank you.'

It was signed, dated and witnessed, and handed to Mary.

'I think the sherry went to your head, Flo,' opined Gladys as they climbed back into the Hot Stompers' van and began battle with the starter. 'How can we possibly put together a whole brass band out of women? Who else plays?'

'What about that Judith Cashmore as lives in Railway Road? I've seen her out playing cornet with the Sally Army.'

'Or used to, before her husband ran off with the captain's wife.'

'What about a conductor? You've got to have one of those.' Alice felt obliged to remind them.

'There's that Lucy Brindle,' suggested Mary. 'She's a really good conductor.'

'Of the Women's Institute choir,' pointed out Gladys scornfully. 'It's not the same thing at all.'

'Her husband plays for Crickleton Colliery,' Florence told them. 'He plays euphonium. She must know summat about brass.'

'Not necessarily.'

'Well ask her,' Alice urged her sister. 'No harm in asking. She can only say no. If she does we can forget the whole thing.'

Chapter 1

But Lucy did not say no. Not right out. Had it been Gladys on the phone when she answered its ring – Gladys the 'awkward customer' – or even Florence, with her outsize personality and big ideas, it is more than likely that she would have batted such a ridiculous suggestion into the waste-paper basket it called for. But the voice on the other end of the phone belonged to Mary. Mary was the youngest and the one who had never known the mother who had died after giving birth to her. Mary had been brought up largely by Alice, the oldest daughter. Moreover, Mary had a son with Down's syndrome. So when she explained to Lucy that the reward for the venture was a van for the handicapped and that only one person had the skill and the expertise to bring their dreams to fruition, Lucy could not bring herself to flatly refuse.

She said that she would look into the matter and let Mary know in a couple of days.

'What's up, love?' Harry wanted to know as his wife wandered thoughtfully back into the kitchen biting her lip, after having replaced the receiver.

'I've just been asked to conduct a Ladies' Brass Band.'

'A Ladies' Brass Band? Which one is that?'

'There isn't one yet.'

'And never will be, neither. Somebody playing silly beggars, was it?'

'I don't think so. She said it was Mary Rawlinson – you know, one of Bill Ainscough's daughters. It did sound like one of

17

the Ainscoughs. Do you think some strange lunatic was having a laugh?'

'Well it wouldn't be a funny one, coming from that direction.' He pulled back his chair and sat down. They were eating at the kitchen table, since there were only the two of them. 'Is that food ready yet?'

Lucy put a warmed plate in front of him and picked up the oven gloves.

'Where would you go looking if you wanted to find women brass players?'

'Dunno. The armed forces – them as used to be in the Women's Royal Army Corps – the WRAF – that sort of thing. If they still play. Women don't stick at things like men do.'

'We get given too many other things to fill our empty little heads with, I suppose.'

'Aye. Important things,' agreed Harry, 'like serving up the tea, for instance.'

Lucy opened the oven grill door and tugged out a tray of sizzling steak.

'Sally Army,' she announced, forking the largest chunk and sliding it carefully on his plate to avoid splashing fat on the table-cloth. She gestured towards the vegetables dishes from which to help himself.

'It looks more like steak to me.'

'I've seen women playing out with the Salvation Army Band. That Charlie Cashmore's wife, for instance. Judith Cashmore. Lives in Railway Road. Has a little daughter.

18

I've seen her out playing cornet.'

'Charlie Cashmore? Him as upped and ran off wi' t'captain's wife?'

'That's the one.'

'Depends what you want to play,' Harry observed, pulling a dubious face. 'All right for "Onward Christian Soldiers".'

'Hymns would be a start. We could go on from there,' pointed out Lucy.

'Might be best. Play four-part stuff, until you've enough players to extend your range a bit.' Harry decided to take it seriously, feeling confident within himself that there was no possibility of it happening.

They both fell to eating and there was no more conversation other than that of the 'pass the mustard' variety. But it had not left their thoughts.

'I've just remembered something,' Lucy informed her husband as he was picking strands of beef from his teeth and taking in the back page of the national daily while he waited for the second course. 'Didn't your Eileen used to play in the works band when she was a typist in the office at Crickleton?'

'Aye, but that were years ago. That's how she and Tom met. She played tenor horn, he played E flat bass. That was before he moved to percussion.'

'Does she ever do any playing now?'

'I doubt she's blown a note since she and Tom got wed,' Harry told her.

'Maybe she'd like to, now that their children are growing up.'

'Maybe. But what will you do about the basses? You can't expect a woman to play one of those.'

'We've already got a bass trombone.'

'Not the same thing at all. And in any case, how many Florrie Ainscoughs are you going to find?'

'All of them, if they're out there.'

'Love, you're out of your depth. Just phone Mary back and say no.'

Lucy might well have done that, but she was proud of her musicianship. If there was one thing about which she was quite confident, it was that she could conduct. She could follow an orchestral score and played the piano fluently enough to be able to accompany most pieces at sight. She was actually qualified only as a piano teacher, yet it was she who had trained the choir of the Adlington WI when they won the coveted Milligan Cup. She was strict and precise and missed no untoward sound. Nor was she afraid of upsetting people's sensibilities.

If this did not make her popular, it did make her respected.

The next day, she phoned Harry's younger sister Eileen and asked what had happened to the tenor horn she used to play.

'Well, isn't that a funny thing!' exclaimed

her sister-in-law. 'Do you know I haven't touched it for fifteen years, then last term Susie comes home from school telling me she wants to play tenor horn in the school band. Is it the tenor horn season or what?'

So Lucy explained about the Ainscoughs and their search for women brass players in the hope of a van for handicapped children. She and Harry had remembered, she added, that Eileen used to play with Crickleton years ago. 'Did you keep the horn after you married?'

'As it happened yes. For sentimental reasons. It brought us together, you know.'

'So Harry told me.'

'I've nearly given it away a couple of times. But I thought Stuart or Philip might want to learn it one day. Then in comes Susie, out of the blue. "Can I play t'tenor horn?"'

'You've still got it, then?'

'Luckily, yes.'

'So you and Susie could share it between you.'

'I don't know what she'd have to say about that.'

'Come on, Eileen. You're the boss.'

'That's news to me.'

'I'm having a few people round for a try-out on Wednesday. Come along and have a go – just for a bit of fun.'

'I'll see if I can still get any notes out of it first.'

21

'I'll expect you, then.'

Next, Lucy phoned Mary, asked her to bring such players as she could muster to the Brindle household on Wednesday evening. They would make a start with quartets and discuss the matter at length. Then they would take a vote on whether or not to continue looking for others to join them.

So on Wednesday there were six of them in Lucy's parlour and it was a bit of a squeeze. Eileen was first there, flexing her lips and hoping she could still pitch in tune; hoping that there would not be too many top Gs in the horn part; hoping that the trombones would drown her. She was glad when Mary turned up with a euphonium. That at least was in the same section as the horn.

The arrival of the other three Ainscough sisters was evident long before they entered the house. A noisy van ground to a halt with a flurry of gravel. The sound of its engine put Lucy in mind of a bass singer whose voice had long since lost its timbre, but who would still bellow manfully with faltering vocal cords. Voices were raised, doors slammed until you began to wonder how many the vehicle had. A booming laugh could be heard.

'Here comes Florrie,' observed Mary with a smile.

The sisters cascaded into the room with

their three long instrument cases, creating an immediate space problem. Lucy had cleared the sideboard of its china ornaments, but it was still a squeeze at case-opening time.

Eileen knew them well by sight, because they lived further down the Lane from her, but she still marvelled how different the sisters were from one another. Alice was the sort you never noticed and whose name you had difficulty recalling. Her figure had gone by the time she was thirty-five and she worked in the office of the local biscuit factory. But when she put the trombone to her lips, you sat up and took notice.

Gladys was always immaculately turned out, with a corrugated perm and a primly powdered face. She had been her father's favourite and the prettiest of the bunch. Several boys had been interested in her, but none of them had measured up to Bill's standards. Now forty-two and no longer sought-after, she worked as a receptionist to a firm of solicitors in Chorley and thought she could talk posh.

Everything about Florence was larger than life. Seeing she was going to be the tallest, Bill had put her on G bass trombone as soon as she could reach seventh shift, using an old instrument with a handle on the slide. She had a warm, outgoing personality. She worked in the mill.

And now here they were: Alice, Gladys, Florence and Mary in Lucy's parlour, along with Eileen, and where were they going to sit, so's not to get their slides tangled up?

'Can we get the three of you over there in front of the window, facing this way?'

With a careful placement of kitchen chairs, they managed it.

'Eileen and Mary, you'll have to go on t'settee. Can you play like that?'

'I can play,' Mary assured her, falling backwards into its comfy depths. 'I don't know whether I can see the music.'

The centre of the room was taken up with open music stands. Lucy would have to conduct from the doorway.

'Where are the cornets going to go?'

'Cornet,' corrected Lucy.

Judith Cashmore had not arrived. Help!

But a few minutes later there was a gentle knock on the door. Lucy opened it to find standing on the step a thin lady in her early thirties with darkish hair dragged back into a bun. She clutched an old-fashioned cornet case of the half-moon type in one hand and a sheaf of music in the other. A handbag was threatening to slip out from under one arm after the effort of rapping at the door.

'Judith?' Lucy felt it was a safe guess.

The newcomer nodded and was ushered inside. She handed Lucy a couple of

24

arrangements which Bandmaster Parkinson had been kind enough to lend her, was divested of her coat and directed to the only remaining space, on the sofa beside Eileen.

Lucy leafed through the pieces, which were 'Variations on a Hymn Tune' and 'In an April Morning'. She wondered whether to make some kind of speech of welcome. But even as she wrestled mentally with the first sentence, while registering that there were no conductor's parts, Florence came over to grab the pieces of paper. She was hungry for music.

'What's this?' she wanted to know, as she handed out the parts to everybody. '"Eventide"?'

'It's a good one to start with,' volunteered Judith in a timid voice.

'I can't find the conductor's score,' Lucy told her.

'Oh dear. Can't you use a first cornet part? That's what they usually do, I think. It's got some of the other parts cued in,' she explained in apologetic tones.

So much for Lucy's prowess in reading an orchestral score. She saw that they were all waiting for her. The nettle had to be grasped. At least she knew the tune, which was the one commonly used for the hymn 'Abide With Me'. She raised her arms. They gazed back at her with rather scary expressions of trust and brought mouthpieces mouthwards.

'Four in a bar,' Lucy called, 'I'll give you a bar in.'

She beat out four to establish the tempo, before bringing them in with a positive downward sweep of the hand.

Her front parlour was filled with a wonderful beefy sound. The cornet was lost and with it the tune, but the lower parts came out warm and strong and beautifully blended. Judith blew her best, but she was not an assertive person and she had some pretty stiff competition coming from in front of the window.

Lucy cared nothing for the tune. She was quite bowled over by the sound and the feeling of power it gave her to produce it with a flick of the hand. When she expanded the sweep the volume grew and a restraining gesture brought the volume down like the dimming of a light, so responsive were the musicians and so well were they in control of their instruments. An ember of enthusiasm began to glow warmly inside her.

They moved on to 'In an April Morning' and it was just the same. They were all good players. They all read their parts well. There was hardly any need to stop. But Lucy made some stops, anyway; partly because she wanted to hear it again and partly because they would be finished in ten minutes if she could not find some nits to pick. She concentrated on balance. The trombones were

26

made to play pianissimo, while Eileen and Judith were encouraged to blow louder, much to Eileen's discomfiture.

After a while, there was a thumping on the front door and Lucy opened it to admit William, Mary's son, followed by her husband Les. They had come to collect her.

'Cup of tea, anybody?'

There was a general chorus of assent. Lucy took herself off to the kitchen while they packed away their instruments. There was no doubt that they had the potential for a band, but where were they going to find the rest of it?

Eileen followed her, noting that Lucy had already laid everything out in preparation. Tidy-minded, was our Lucy.

'Shall I take in this tray of cups?'

'Yes, if you like. How did you get on?'

'Grand. I couldn't hear myself at all. As far as I could tell I didn't play any wrong notes. Until you spoiled it by making the trombones play soft.'

'I could tell that it threw you. But don't worry. You weren't so bad considering you haven't played for so long. I know you'll improve.'

They marched laden into the parlour and handed out slices of cake.

'Right. Well. You're the experts,' Lucy assured the trombonists. 'What do you reckon?'

'Smashing,' Florrie told her. 'But we're not a band. We need twenty cornets and a big bass drum.'

'And somewhere to practise.'

'I do need help,' Judith admitted. 'Can I bring my daughter next time? She's only nine, but she's been playing for two years. She's getting along really well. She can manage a second cornet part.'

'Oh. Yes. Please bring her along.'

Florrie took a slurp of tea and wiped her mouth with a tissue.

'That's the best time I've had for ages,' she told Lucy, as people began to stand up ready to go. 'I've got an idea for a practice room. Do you want to leave it with me and I'll get back to you?'

'Yes please.'

Mary and Les drove home. William was humming his own private music in the back of the car.

'You look brighter than I've seen you for a long time,' Les told her.

'I enjoyed it.'

Mary thought about her Van for the Handicapped. It represented a degree of freedom. It stood for hope of better things. Everybody needs hope. That is why so many people bet on the horses, buy raffle tickets, play bingo.

Chapter 2

'Two cornets!' cried Harry incredulously, pulling off his trousers before removing his socks and thus getting them stuck on his ankles. He sat on the bed and wrestled with the problem. 'Two cornets and one of them a little lass? You'll need at least ten with all that weight in the middle.'

The bed sagged as he rolled backwards and tugged the second trouser leg until his foot was free.

'That's an improvement on Florrie's estimate, anyway.'

Lucy brushed out her white hair in front of the mirror. Creases ran from her nose to the corners of her mouth. Did she spend too much time pursing her lips?

'And you'll have to find somewhere else to practise.'

'That goes without saying, Harry.'

The next day at teatime, Lucy phoned Eileen.

'Where can we get some more cornets from?'

'Cornets or cornet players?'

'Players, of course.'

29

'I wasn't going to suggest it,' suggested Eileen, 'but the Hetherington girls two doors down from us play cornet. I know they do. I should do. The whole family plays summat. But you'll have to ask them, not me. We're not on speaking terms.'

'Really?'

'Really.'

Lucy kept an encouraging silence, but Eileen would not elucidate.

Babylon Lane was the name of the road where Eileen and Tom Riley lived. Also the Ainscoughs. This did not mean that they lived on top of one another. It was a long lane that wound all the way up from Adlington to Heath Charnock, starting at a busy crossing and shopping centre where it met the main road to Chorley. It stretched uphill to a high windy point known as the Bay Horse, after the pub which stood there, commanding a splendid view of the Anglezarke moors, which filled the north-east horizon with a dramatic skyline culminating in the shoulder of Winter Hill.

The rows of terraced houses which clung to the sides of the lane had stunning views of half the mill chimneys in south west Lancashire on the one hand and of wilderness on the other. But both went unnoticed by the vast majority of householders. They only knew it was cold when the wind blew and very steep, whether you were going up or down.

The community spirit in the Lane was quite strong. The days when a fine morning might find the women out putting donkey stone on the front doorstep while they had a gossip were a thing of the past. But you could still have a natter in the greengrocer's or borrow a cup of flour from a neighbour.

The Rileys and the Hetheringtons lived two doors apart about half way up, on a bend often referred to as decibel corner; not just because of the brass-playing families. It was also the spot at which heavy lorries tended to change gear.

Eileen put the phone down from speaking to Lucy and returned to the kitchen, whence she was about to serve the tea to her family. She was a slim and energetic woman, with a fluffy blonde perm. Always busy.

'Still going on about that band, are you?' Tom called to her. He was hungry and wanted his tea. 'Haven't you given up yet? I've told you. You'll never get a bass.'

'Give us a bit more time, will you?'

'They're looking for someone to play bass at school,' Susie came out with suddenly, as she carefully picked up the pile of dishes from where they were warming on top of the cooker. The menfolk took their places at the table. 'Jimmy Allen's given up.'

'He must have seen you coming, Susie!'

yelled Philip.

'Don't be rude!' snapped Susie and gave him the chipped plate.

'Bass?' Eileen switched off the cooker.

'E flat bass. Like Dad used to play. Not the big one.'

Eileen hunted for the oven gloves. Bass player! What luck! If Susie could get put onto that – and she already knew the fingering, which was the same as for the tenor horn – they would have another much-needed instrument for the band.

'What you doing in there?' came Tom's voice from the next room. 'Have you gone on strike?'

'Striking is for *men*,' retorted Eileen, as Susie returned and handed her the double oven gloves she had been looking for. She put them on and took out of the oven a large earthenware dish full of hotpot. 'Women are what you can't manage without.'

On Saturday morning, Lucy had the call from Florence that she had been hoping for.

'We can have the back room at t'Spinners. It's all fixed.'

'Spinners?'

'Spinners Arms. Corner of Railway Road. It's got plenty of space for folk to park, and he's willing to let us have it on Wednesday evenings. We could even walk it, if the van packs up. So can Eileen. So can Judith. It's that close.'

'Thank you Florence, I'm really pleased,' said Lucy. 'It somehow makes us more of a band, if we've got a band room.'

The Hetherington girls had been recruited, which pretty well ruled out a front-parlour assembly.

'He wants to charge us ten shillings a time,' added Florence, saving the bad news for the end. 'Can we afford it?'

'I'll put it to everybody. Try it once and then take a vote on it. I'll get as many players as I can for next Wednesday, anyway.'

'We might beat him down to seven and sixpence, I reckon.'

When Harry had had his tea that evening Lucy told him she had found some more players.

'It looks like there might be ten of us, if Susie starts on bass. Can you find us a bit of music with more parts – and a proper conductor's score if they have such things?'

'Ten players? In our front parlour?'

'No. At the Spinners. We've got their back room. For Wednesdays.'

Harry looked dubious, but he came back from work on Monday with a piece called 'The Old Castle', which was scored for full band, but without much solo work. It was not difficult to play. He put the music down on the kitchen table and fanned out the separate parts so that she could see how many there were.

'Soprano cornet? What's that?'

'There you are, you see. Better take a look through. See what a real band is made of.'

His tone was kind, but she still felt condescended to. A real band, indeed! She counted the number of parts and it came to eighteen, with the percussion.

'Don't forget,' added Harry, just to ward off any complacency, 'that a good band will often have more than one player to a part, especially with the cornets and basses.'

'We can work on that later,' said Lucy. But she felt depressed. She could not see how they would ever be in a position to enter a contest, let alone score more than a well-established band like Great Hulme Motors. But she gathered up the parts and put them in their folder. There was no harm in carrying on with the players she had, as long as they were prepared to come along and play.

On Wednesday there were nine of them there. Susie had not yet got her hands on the E flat bass, but was confident that she would. There were enough chairs for them all and they had been warned to bring their own music stands. The Ainscoughs were already putting out chairs in what, after some argument, they considered to be the right placing, as Lucy walked in. She surveyed the room. It

34

was nicely decorated, not too cold and rather big, which left room for the expansion of their numbers which she hoped would occur. Judith arrived with Wendy, a small girl with round National Health spectacles in front of large intelligent eyes. Her hair was tied back in neat little pigtails.

The new band room was ideal for them. They only had a short walk uphill from their terraced house in Railway Road.

'Do you want the cornets this side, Lucy?' called Gladys. 'And the trombones in the middle?'

'Don't be daft!' That was Florence, of course. 'You want trombones on your left and horns in t'middle.'

'What horns?'

Lucy saw that she would have to make a quick decision, be it right or wrong.

'I'll have the cornets over here on the left, I think. Trombones just go where you feel most comfortable. Eileen and Mary can take the space that's left over. That's just for now, of course.'

The door opened and a man in a flat cap came in, leading two teenage girls. He saw Lucy was holding a sheaf of music and came across.

'Are you Mrs Brindle? We spoke on the phone.'

'Mr Hetherington, I presume.'

They shook hands.

'This is Rachel and Rebecca.'

The two girls sported short and sensible haircuts, sensible jumpers and skirts, Rachel, the elder one, was a little overweight, while Rebecca, being almost fourteen, had the skinny limbs of one who was in the process of shooting upwards in height.

Lucy smiled at them and they dutifully returned her smile.

'What time shall I come and pick them up?' he wanted to know.

'Oh Dad!' hissed Rachel, cringing a little. She was fifteen. 'It's only up the road.'

Put in his place, he left and the two girls opened their cases and took out their instruments in well-trained silence.

'Cornets over this side,' Lucy told them. 'Next to Mrs Cashmore, here, and Wendy. Wendy is going to take second cornet part. Can you play first, Rachel?'

'I'm not a cornet,' Rachel told her. There was a slight note of scorn in her voice.

Help! thought Lucy, glancing at the instrument in Rachel's hand. It was larger than the other cornets, now she came to look at it properly. But she could not for the life of her think what it was.

'That's a flugelhorn,' Alice came to her rescue. She saw Lucy's uncertainty. 'Put her next to your tenor horn,' she advised. 'For now.'

When Mary arrived a few moments later,

their numbers had reached the allotted nine. Lucy stared at the full score of 'The Old Castle' as Wendy handed the parts round. Everything except the bass trombone was written in the treble clef – even the basses! Not that they had any basses, but it was a bit disconcerting. Not like an orchestral score. And what was repiano cornet for exactly? Should she put Wendy or Rebecca on repiano? She was going to have to learn as she went along.

She raised her smart new baton, caught their eyes and brought it down.

Well, nobody could say the sound was quite adequate. There were noticeable gaps in places. The balance was still in favour of the lower end. The flugel player seemed to be under-employed, unless she was missing bits out.

But on the plus side, the cornet line was much improved and when the time came to call a halt nobody wanted to stop.

'We're running close to Christmas,' Lucy addressed them as they laid their instruments into cases and clicked them shut. 'I want to use the break to look for some more players, so go home and keep practising. I'll expect to see every one of you back here the first week in January.'

There were disappointed groans.

'I know it's a shame to stop, but if any of you have got suggestions to make or problems to raise, now is the time.'

'What do you say we advertise for some more players?' suggested Alice. 'We could try the *Chorley Guardian*.'

'That's right,' agreed Florence. 'We could use some of the money we collected playing carols.'

'I don't mind paying for an advert,' protested Alice. 'Not just the once.'

At this point, Mary asked to be allowed to say a few words. She was not a person who readily addressed an assembly or pushed herself forwards. But she felt the occasion demanded it. She hooked some of her dark fine hair behind one ear, clasped her hands in front of her and swallowed nervously.

'I suppose you all know that we're doing this in an effort to get a van so that we can take out children like William – or with any kind of handicap. Give them a treat. Let them meet one another and play together. I want you to know that I appreciate the effort you're all putting in. If you enjoy it too – well, it's no more than you deserve.'

She looked as if she wanted to continue, but could not find the right words, so Lucy led the applause, allowing her a dignified exit.

Each one packed away her instrument and departed, calling 'Merry Christmas' to everyone else. They were still at it out in the car park, and the night echoed with seasonal good wishes, as Lucy brought up the rear, making sure everything was left in good order.

William and Les were waiting outside in the car when Mary joined them. She gave William the euphonium to hold and climbed in, clutching the handbag which still held the precious promise signed by Eddie Pickerskill.

Chapter 3

Winter entered into the spirit of Christmas by gifting the populace some fine weather during the last week of December, which meant that those who had eaten too many roast potatoes or too much pudding could enjoy a brisk hike up Rivington Pike to work off some of the excess fat, should they wish to do so.

Not many took up the option.

But even so, none of Lucy's recruits was stricken by seasonal flu as yet. So the first Wednesday in January found the same people at the same place. The advertisement for players had been drafted and was due to appear soon. No progress had been made on the bass, because the schools had been on holiday.

The trombones made their usual well-blended sound. Rachel and Rebecca were in good lip. Their dad kept them up to the mark. They had spent a lot of time playing quartets together as a family with brother Daniel, who took the lower part on trombone. Young Wendy was now sitting beside her mother to add her weight to the melody line and it helped more than Lucy had expected. But even so, more power was still needed in that corner.

They spent most of the time on 'The Old Castle'. At first they concentrated on becoming familiar with every last turret. But as those present were beginning to master it and Lucy was finding her way more easily through her first full score, she realised more and more just how much she needed some extra players if it was to sound as it was meant to sound. There was one passage in particular that needed three tenor horns, two baritones and a euphonium.

When the last parp had issued forth, instruments had been packed away and cases snapped shut, Lucy sought out Judith. She found her packing her cornet away, Wendy standing quietly by her side, her cornet case held in both hands. They were two slight and somehow vulnerable figures, who kept close together for mutual support in a tough world.

'Are there any other ladies in the Salvation

Army as might like to join us?'

'Not in our particular division, unless you want tambourines.'

'It wasn't what I had in mind.'

Lucy thought of Harry's remark about 'Onward Christian Soldiers'. Tambourines would play right into the hands of the scoffers.

'What about school?' she persevered. 'Are there any girls in your school who can play brass instruments?'

'I think most of the girls go for clarinets and flutes. But I'm not sure.' Judith finished struggling with the fastenings of her case and picked up her handbag. 'The choir is my department.'

'I must get some players from somewhere,' Lucy gazed around the emptying room. She spotted Mary. 'What's happened to that advert in the *Chorley Guardian?* I haven't seen it. Has it been in?'

'Should be out by this weekend.'

There were three replies.

A seventeen-year-old by the name of Sheena Grimshaw still had the baritone horn she used to play in the school band and felt like 'a bit of a blow' now and again.

Winifred, the second caller, was the war widow of a pilot. The two children she had struggled to bring up alone were now independent. She had played the tenor horn in the WRAF band. She was rusty but had time on her hands. Would she do?

She most certainly would.

There were several hoaxes from giggling girls or thirteen-year-old boys who wanted to make suggestive remarks or rude noises down the phone. Finally a man phoned.

'Harold Mackenzie here,' he announced. 'Are you the lady with the brass band?'

'Speaking.'

He wanted to know where they met and when. Lucy told him but felt she had to add, 'It's a ladies' band. It's not for men.'

'Glad to hear it,' he said and hung up.

Lucy decided it was a hoax from somebody with a rather unfunny sense of humour. So she was not expecting it when at the next practice a prosperous-looking gentleman of about forty with thinning fair hair walked through the door and stood watching them, making no attempt either to sit down or to leave. It was distracting. 'The Old Castle' was in danger of crumbling to a halt, so she shored it up with a temporary halt and challenged the intruder.

'Can I help you?'

'My wife plays trumpet,' he told her. 'Any good to you?'

'We can give her a try,' said Lucy carefully, assuming he meant cornet and not trumpet. Most people failed to differentiate between the two.

He disappeared. Lucy caught Eileen's eye and they exchanged we've-got-a-right-one-here faces. But in about thirty seconds he was back with his wife.

Annette had green eyes, abundant dark auburn hair, fine facial bones, long legs and a perfect figure. She carried in her hand a trumpet case of the finest make and, although her clothes were obviously toned down for the occasion, they still looked like something out of *Vogue* magazine.

There was absolute silence in the hall. You could have heard a sheet of music drop. She always had that effect on people. When she walked into a party the men stopped discussing the best bet for the three thirty and sidled over, leaving their womenfolk to grit their teeth and urge each other to have another piece of stuffed celery.

'Do you want me to stay, sweetie?' he asked her.

'No, darling. You go and have a drink. Come back for me in an hour or so.'

She set the seal on her words with a wifely peck on his cheek and he left.

Lucy gestured to her to sit by Judith. It was a gleaming trumpet of an expensive make which she drew from the case. A couple of mutes and a mouthpiece brush could also be glimpsed nestling in a side pocket of the red plush case interior. Florence raised her eyebrows and dropped her mouth. Up until now her American B flat and F trombone had been the best instrument in the room.

Annette hid her nerves with the poise which came naturally to her. She would spend hours at home going through page after page of the exercise book, which Harold had hoped would keep her out of mischief. But she had never played in the company of others. She had no idea how she would measure up to them. She gazed at the page she was sharing with Judith. There did not seem to be anything to be afraid of.

Lucy brought the baton down and for the first time heard the melody plainly. The brilliant tone of the trumpet cut through the mellowness of the rest of the band. It may not have suited the purist, but it would, Lucy told herself, do for now. She beamed at Annette gratefully and reached for an arrangement called 'Regimental Selection' which, Harry had assured her, was very popular with his colliery band.

The horn section was much improved, now that there was an experienced tenor in Winifred to support Eileen, and a baritone in Sheena. It only needed a second baritone and a third tenor to be complete, though Eileen was, not surprisingly, weak on the solo part. Winifred would probably have been better in that position had her lips been twenty years younger.

Lucy did not know what to make of

Sheena. The girl had turned up late carrying a baritone horn in a battered case which was coming unstitched along the seams. Her skirt was too short and too tight. She wore thick make-up – surely not needed at her age! She was pretty enough – if you did not look at Annette. But there was something of the ill-kempt about her.

However, she played like someone who knew what she was doing. In the few places where the baritone sound was meant to be predominant, her sound was there, predominating. What more could be asked?

For the first part of the evening, at least, she made a good job of her part. At the mid-session break which Lucy gave them to rest their embouchures, she started to pack away her baritone. But when she saw that the others just sat and relaxed instead of going home, she lit a cigarette and blew smoke over everybody. By the end of the evening she was restless and inattentive and when the thunder of a motorbike announced itself in the car park, she packed up her baritone with a muttered excuse and left. How she could balance on the back of a bike holding the bulky baritone horn and wearing that skirt was beyond Lucy's imaginings.

Shortly after that, Harold Mackenzie returned and distracted them all by standing near the doorway with his hands in his pockets. Annette started to make silly mistakes and Judith had to carry the melody again. Finally, Les came in with William, who tried to sing along with the tune. Although they could have continued for another five minutes, Lucy decided enough was enough for now and called a halt.

It had been an encouraging practice, but still far from satisfactory, which was the verdict she passed on to Harry as she cleared away the tea dishes.

'I expect most of them are out of practice,' he commented, without having listened very closely. 'There's nothing to worry about there. Personally I'm staggered that you're doing so well. I'd have thought you'd have given up by now. Still,' he added, opening out his newspaper as a sign that he was hoping to end the conversation, 'there's plenty of time for that.'

'When are you going to come and listen in, Dad?' Mary asked on one of her regular visits to her father.

'Nay, you wouldn't want me listening,' he told her. 'I might say summat you wouldn't like.'

He and Mary had always crossed swords. Somehow his disappointment that she was a girl had been greater than for any of the others. She had been his last chance. She had been the final straw that finished off his wife. Not that either of them had ever admitted any animosity towards each other, even to themselves.

'Well maybe you're missing a treat,' she rallied to their defence. 'We enjoy it anyway.'

'A women's band!' he spat into the fire. 'Monkey's tea-party, more like.'

'Less of that!' Alice told him tartly, coming in with a pot of tea and some cups on a tray. 'You'd be surprised. We'll make you eat those words.'

She handed him a sandwich on a plate.

He lifted a corner of the bread as though expecting to find his words staring back at him.

'Do you know someone called Eddie Pickerskill?' Alice continued as she poured out tea into their cups.

'Oh aye. Don't mention that name when Alf's here, will you? He'll tell you a thing or two.'

'What'll he tell us?'

'Cornet player, Eddie used to be. Played top cornet for Great Hulme Motors.'

'Is he rich?'

'Aye, like as not. Started selling second-hand cars after the war. Did very well for himself. He used to be just a factory hand like everybody else. Got put to work on the lorries in the army during the war. Learned a thing or two there, I suppose. But he got too close to a bomb one dark night. Ruined his hearing.'

47

'So what happened? Could he not play then?'

'That's right. He couldn't. Trouble was, he thought he could. He wasn't stone deaf. Just tone deaf. They kept trying nicely to persuade him to go. He got put further and further down the cornets. When he finally reached third cornet he dug his heels in and refused. Can't blame him, in a way. He used to play all the show pieces – you know, "Carnival of Venice", "The Nightingale". That stuff. Third cornet was a bit of an insult, like.'

'Could they not have put him on bass or summat?'

'Bass? You can still ruin a band on bass, you know.' He took a last drag from the half-inch of cigarette in his arthritic fingers and flicked it into the fire to join his phlegm there. 'Nay, they got a bit too brutal in the end. Told him to go. He took it badly.'

'How long ago was that then?' Mary wanted to know.

'Ee, I dunno. I think you were still at school.'

Obviously the iron – if not the brass – had entered his soul.

Aunt Charity, who was partly paralysed, was sitting at the table by the window, engaging William in a game of cards. Handicapped people tend to be like the furniture. You forget they are there. But unlike furniture, they have the power of speech.

'Florrie says he's going to buy you a van,' she came out with, letting William have the Jack of Diamonds, because he liked it. 'Is that true?'

'I've got the paper to prove it,' Mary told her, patting her handbag.

'It's got to be earned,' Alice reminded her. 'There's some work needs putting in first.'

'If you get it,' called Charity, 'will you take me to Blackpool?'

'Nay, what do you want to go there for?'

'I've never been on t'Big Dipper. That's what I've always wanted. To go on t'Big Dipper.'

'You'd be frightened to death,' Bill told her.

'Me and Les'll take you anyway,' Mary promised her. 'We'll take you next summer. We'll all go on t'Dipper.'

They laughed, knowing the Big Dipper was a safe distance away, not knowing that to Charity it represented all the experiences in life which she would never have.

Chapter 4

As the New Year progressed, a cold wind set in, with a few dashes of sleet. The dawns were at their darkest, making it a miserable experience to set out on a January morning,

49

when the sun had not yet hauled itself above the horizon, the streets were black and bleak, the pavements were either wet or icy and as often as not a chill wind numbed the nose.

Judith and Wendy walked together down the road, the headlights of the oncoming cars flicking over them as they passed. The Junior School actually looked a cheerful haven, with its lit windows and promise of warmth. Judith saw her daughter safely into the playground, before trudging further onwards to Adlington Secondary Modern. She felt her heart sinking at the sight of the grey stone gateposts. A trickle of unruly children jostled towards the door. Insolence was in the air; none of it tempered at the sight of Judith. She was even jostled herself on the main staircase by one of the boys whose 'friend' had attempted to trip him on the top step.

'Sorry miss...'

Then he saw it was only Judith and they scuttled away snickering. There were times when she did not know how she was going to get through the next twenty years.

'You've got to stand up to them,' said Mavis Fielding later in the staff room. 'Show the little blighters who's boss.'

Judith was silent. If she had had a tenth of Mavis's personality she might have tried. But she was a failure and the children knew it. Everybody knew it. She could not keep her man. She was boring in bed. No wonder they felt nothing but contempt for her.

She had to play the piano for assembly again, since the senior pupil the task was normally allotted to was absent. Her small hands thumped down on the keys as hard as they could, to make the poor instrument heard at the back of the hall. The singing was insipid and you could hear alternative versions of the words from certain quarters. The militant left at this time was pressing to do away with religious assembly. They saw it as 'conditioning' the children. But if this was indoctrination then she was Karl Marx.

Most of the morning Judith spent trying to persuade form three to make a glad sound in some English folk songs. They found the words silly, of course. The boys fooled about and showed off in front of the girls. She would have to look in the catalogues for something a bit more modern.

By the mid-morning break the recent Christmastide was already a distant vista fading into the mist of the past, while Easter was not yet even a dot on the horizon of the future.

Collecting a coffee in the staff room, she remembered Lucy's request for players from the school. She had little to do with the school band. The new music teacher was popular with staff and pupils alike. He was good looking and full of enthusiasm and

51

often the centre of jovial groups. He was everything that Judith was not. She was scared of him. He was a bit condescending towards Judith, whom he thought of as a poor helpless female; which, in fact, she was.

However, she must do her bit for Lucy. It was, after all, in a good cause. She looked around for Joe Greenhalgh, as he was called.

'Who came off best, then?' he wanted to know as she took the chair next to his, 'The lower third or Vaughan Williams?'

'You heard them, did you?' Judith coloured up a little in shame. 'It certainly wasn't Vaughan Williams.'

'Little beggars have got no soul,' he said kindly. 'You're wasted on them.'

'It's a minority, really. I expect they enjoy wind band more.'

'Make more noise too. Why is it the troublemakers always seem to end up on trombone?'

'What about horns and baritones? Do you have many horn and baritone players?'

'Of course, you play brass, don't you? Care to sit in with us?'

Judith was appalled by the thought.

'That's very kind of you. I expect you have enough cornets.'

'There's always room for good players.'

'We're a bit short of baritones and basses and cornets in our band,' she persevered.

'We don't use baritones much. Hardly

need them in a wind band. There's a couple of boys on euphs. You can play a baritone part on a euphonium.'

'That's true, though the tone isn't the same.'

'You're might. Still, I'm sure they'd help you out if you're stuck. Like me to ask them?'

'No. Please don't bother. It's a women's band.' She was surprised to find him such a kind man. He treated her as though she mattered. He had the sort of strong shoulder you could fall upon and sob out your troubles; a lapel that would feel comforting against your cheek; a hand gentle in your hair...

Judith called a horrified halt to her train of thought. She had to take the senior choir next. She contemplated that until all romantic thoughts vanished like the smoke of an illicit cigarette through a toilet window.

'What's this repiano cornet part?' Lucy asked Harry, as she was leafing through 'The Old Castle' score prior to the Wednesday evening practice. 'What's it for, exactly? It just seems to be the same as first cornet – most of it. Just how important is it?'

'If you put someone on it, then you'll find out,' Harry told her. He was heartily sick of the subject, especially as her questions were now beginning to tax his own knowledge, which was not by any means comprehensive.

'That's just it. I can't really spare anyone, except when they're all there, which hasn't happened yet.'

'It's a kind of back-up. It often shares with the flugel. Didn't you say you'd got a flugel?'

'Yes, I've got a flugel.'

'Well just tell her to play everything in her part, whether it says rep or flugel. There you are. Problem solved.'

His tone was impatient. He had had a tiring day at work. A sore throat and the sniffs warned him he might be getting a cold. Moreover, he had just had the bill for the rates.

Lucy was not entirely happy with Harry's suggestion. She had already noticed that Rachel was prone to leaving out difficult bits or high notes. But she would take his advice for now. It was not a good time to persist.

On Friday, as usual, Florrie took Auntie Charrers for their weekly evening at the Spinners Arms. Charity had had polio as a girl and it had left her half-paralysed. Being the strongest, Florence was the sister given the task of helping her aunt in and out of the wheelchair and taking her around. She did not mind. They both liked a good laugh and enjoyed one another's company.

The downhill walk with the wheelchair did not take long, since the pub, as Flo had explained to Lucy, was situated at the top of

Railway Road, within trombone earshot of the lower reaches of Babylon Lane.

She installed Charity in the lounge bar and bought her a sherry, together with a half of Guinness for herself. They sipped and chatted with their fellow regulars. Then somebody started to thump on the piano and several voices quavered into song. Florrie was persuaded to do her Gracie Fields impression with 'The Biggest Aspidistra in the World', after which she stood behind the wheelchair while she and Charity raised their voices for 'Bless This House' in harmony. Charity's mouth drooped at the corners when she sang. She looked as though she was about to burst into tears. In fact it was the highlight of her week.

Eventually, 'time' was called. People finished their drinks and sauntered out of the door with varying degrees of steadiness. As Florrie was about to manoeuvre the wheelchair over the high step of the Spinners and out into the night, she heard a voice behind her shoulder say:

'Here, let me do that for you.'

There stood little Wilfred Robinson, widowed last year and still moping.

'It's no trouble, Wilfred.'

'Come on now. I don't like to see a lassie doing the hard work.'

Lassie!

Florence was so flattered that she let him

55

take the handle. Of course, the chair went with a bump, taking him with it and carrying him half way across the parking ground before Charity took pity on him and slammed the brakes on. He ran into it, knocking out his dentures.

Florrie held onto the doorpost and gasped for breath. She wanted to laugh so much that only a high-pitched wheeze came out and tears began to run down her face.

'I've lost my front teeth.' He was down on his hands and knees in the dark. A car was turning and he was terrified, not that it would run over him, but that it might run over his teeth.

'Help me. Help me find my teeth.'

'Here!' shouted Charity to the car driver, keeping her presence of mind. 'Lights this way, please.'

The obliging driver turned so that they were bathed in light, creating a blacker shadow around their feet. The driver got out and Florrie came to help too, fighting back mirth. Never a smile crossed Charity's face. She directed the search imperiously from her wheelchair, leaning forwards to peer at the ground.

'It's no good, Mr Robinson,' she had to say eventually. 'We'll have to come and hunt again tomorrow when it's light.'

He turned on them a toothless gape of black despair, looking so much like something from a horror film, lit from below, that Florence was consumed with laughter again. The car driver climbed back into his car and Charity leaned back in her chair. Then she gave a shriek.

'There's something sticking in me back!'

So Wilfred found his teeth and helped push Charity up the Lane and they laughed and sang all the way.

On Monday after work Florence was fighting her usual way across to her bus queue when she heard a voice.

'How do Florrie, not speaking today?'

'Hey up! It's him with the teeth!'

Heads turned throughout the length and breadth of the crowded bus station.

'Got time for a cup of tea?' he called.

'No. But let's have one anyway.'

They missed their bus, and rather than wait any longer, they walked the two miles home through the blustery evening, not noticing the odd dash of rain. Half way back Wilfred's shoelace broke. He bent to tie the ends, leaning against the lamp post, and when he straightened he hit his head on the shoulder-high litter bin, knocking it crooked in its bracket, so that it tipped and showered him with sweet papers, cigarette packets and apple comes, as well as objects it was better not to examine too closely.

'Everything happens to you, Wilfred,'

sobbed Florrie, when she could speak again.

At four o'clock one afternoon, Lucy and Eileen sat in Tessa's Tea Rooms in Chorley, with cups of tea and Eccles cakes. They often went shopping together and ended up surrounded by their purchases, resting their feet and replacing their energy with the cup that cheers.

'That Sheena,' began Eileen, breaking off a piece of cake and putting it into her mouth, because it was more ladylike than taking a large bite and having a flight of crumbs alight on her bosom, 'she's not that Len Grimshaw's lass, is she?'

'You tell me,' Lucy told her. Eileen was always more clued up than she was with all the gossip, living as she did halfway up Babylon Lane. It was tantamount to having a tap on the main line of communications. 'What Len Grimshaw, anyway?'

'Lives down by t'canal. Him as is always being picked up drunk.'

'Oh him. That Grimshaw!'

'His wife disappeared ten years ago. They say he used to beat her.'

Lucy stirred her tea and digested the thought. It was harder to stomach than the Eccles cake. Suddenly Sheena's tight skirt and heavy make-up were no longer something to smile at.

'Is that just rumour, or do you know it for

a fact?'

'What does anybody know for a fact?'

Or what does anyone care, thought Lucy, if it makes a good story?

Sheena woke with a pounding headache. The sound of a motor bike in warm-up throttle was attacking her through the window. Window? She opened her eyes and hurriedly closed them again. As the bike gave a mighty snarl and began to fade into the distance, she tried to remember how she came to be in this strange bed. She hauled herself out of it and staggered to the toilet.

It was a while before she felt ready to emerge, shaky but with less of a head. She shivered and began the hunt for her clothes. They were well distributed all over the place. It was like playing 'hunt the thimble' on a grand scale.

However, after half an hour or more she was fully clad, except for her left shoe, which no amount of searching revealed. So she padded barefoot into the kitchen – then wished she hadn't; for when she switched the light on all manner of tiny creatures scuttled in panic to safety under the cooker and fridge. She picked her way gingerly across the less disgusting areas until she found some congealed coffee powder in the bottom of a jar.

There was nothing in the fridge except ice.

She switched the machine off and left it to defrost at leisure. Clear that up, Steve!

She opened the front door in the hope of finding some milk. There was none, but her left shoe was lying there, half full of rain.

She forced some coffee down, did her hair in the upstairs mirror and applied some make-up. Then, donning her soggy shoes and desperately late for work, she clicked and clacked down the lane and into redundancy.

'Anyone know where Sheena is?' Lucy addressed the room in general, as they were assembling minus their baritone horn player, on the next drizzly Wednesday evening.

'Does anyone ever know where Sheena is?' someone muttered.

'She had the sack on Monday,' volunteered Rachel.

'Anyone seen her since?'

'None of us lives near t'canal.'

'We'll start without her then. Let's have a look at the "Medley of Scottish Airs". Have you all got your parts?'

There was a general murmur of interest as they examined the music on their stands. This was one they had not tried before. It was basically fairly simple, but had two cadenzas. The first was for solo cornet and the other for euphonium and they both needed experienced players to carry them off. It had only just occurred to Lucy that they could be missed out.

'You can leave out the cadenzas for now. So ignore any pauses you come across. Just carry on as if they weren't there.'

She gave them a few seconds to note where the pauses were that they had to ignore and raised her baton, caught their collective eye and made the downbeat. They were off, like a moving vehicle that gathered momentum, and travelled, shakily perhaps, along its given track in pursuit of its appointed destination. It had to be brought screeching to a halt at the second double bar because of some untoward noises in the cornets.

Once the brass had sporadically ceased, however, it was evident that most of the interference was coming from outside. A revving and a roaring filled the air, accompanied by thick blue fumes which poured through the doorway as Sheena burst in. A fearful crescendo followed as the source of the racket reversed and gathered power. Only when it disappeared up the road did the noise diminish in a merciful morendo.

'Sorry I'm late. I got a lift on Steve's bike,' she flung out to the room in general, drawing her instrument out of its case.

'So that's what it was.'

'We thought the Martians had landed,' added Eileen.

Lucy regarded Sheena carefully as the girl

took her place. She felt a little concerned about her, knowing what she now knew. She was not sure that all that eye shadow was, in fact, eye shadow. Still, she would get no thanks for interfering. All she could do was be patient with her and try to make her feel the valued member of the band which she actually was.

Her resolve was soon put to the test. While Sheena put up her music stand, Mary found the first baritone part for 'Scottish Airs' and laid it ready.

'Let's start again from the top,' said Lucy, 'and make a note that we're in two sharps. I don't want to hear so many C naturals this time, please.'

She brought the baton down and the locomotive started up again, more smoothly this time, but with a disconcerting bubbling sound. Lucy stopped them and waited while Sheena opened her water key. A substantial amount of water hit the floor. Lucy sighed and started them again and this time Sheena redeemed herself by making quite a good sound. The baritone bridged the gap between the tenors and the euphonium, giving the section more substance. When Sheena concentrated she could produce the goods. Somewhere in that wayward girl a musician was struggling to get out.

Chapter 5

The month of March arrived and with it the annual South Lancashire Festival of Brass. Next year Lucy's band would hope to compete in the event against Great Hulme Motors, should they succeed in putting together a full band. Of course, Lucy had been along in the past on the Saturday night, to support Harry and the Crickleton Colliery Band.

This year, however, she wanted to watch the whole festival. She wanted to view it with a more critical eye so that she could form a better opinion as to the standard required; also as to what went down well from an audience's point of view and what did not.

The Thursday and the Friday were taken up mostly with solo performers and small groups – duets, trios, quartets and even quintets. There were several classes, divided by size, or by age – the junior bands played in the afternoon. Marching bands formed one class, there was a section for religious music, for small bands and for the full-size Works' Bands – the climax of the event and the real excitement. It took place on the Saturday, when the working men were free to lock horns as rival bands. The winner in this category would usually go on to enter the National Championships at the Albert Hall in October.

Lucy juggled around some of her piano pupils to make time to attend the festival on the Thursday and the Friday. She wanted to look at the solo classes this year. She scanned the programme for girls' names. They were few and far between. There was, however, a girl of eleven who came third in the 10–14-year-old class. She played a soprano cornet. An older girl did not do quite so well on euphonium, but well enough to hold down a second baritone part, Lucy felt sure. But even in the adult classes there were no female bass players. Not one!

On Saturday Eileen joined her and they took their seats in a packed auditorium, glad to have booked them in advance, since there were none spare. The sense of excited anticipation was almost palpable. The curtains drew apart to general applause and conversation had to cease. Spread across the stage before them was the magnificent sight of a full working man's band in their red and gold uniforms. The gleaming brass took the spotlight and threw it back again in all directions. The baton went down and the sound sprang forth every bit as bold and colourful as the picture it was projected from. There was nothing, Lucy decided, quite like it.

Crickleton placed second to the Aviation Band – one of the leading bands in the country. Lucy did not envy the adjudicator his task. She had to admit that she would have found it difficult to choose between one band and the next. It took some time to train the ear to the nuances of timbre and the workings of the inner parts, which, along with general attack and polish, distinguish the good from the excellent.

Great Hulme Motors were in a lesser category, but they were still going to be a force to be reckoned with. For a start, they had many players which Lucy lacked. They had a soprano, three tenors and two each of baritone and euphonium, and four strong basses, as well as a percussionist who played fit to drown the rest, which might cover a multitude of faults. As it happened the adjudicator was aware of that ploy and took some points off them because the drums made too much noise.

Producing a band fit to measure up to all that was going to be difficult for Lucy, but not impossible. She noted down the name of every woman performer in the solo and small ensemble classes. Most of them were likely to live some distance away, but she could try to borrow them for the odd occassion. If they could be here this year, they could be here next year too.

Sunday brought a foretaste of spring to Lancashire's winter-weary denizens. The sun came out in the afternoon and blazed upon hillside and reservoir as if it had got off at the wrong stop.

There was a knock on the Ainscoughs' door.

'It's a feller for Florrie.'

A feller for Florrie!

'Tell him to come in,' shouted old Bill without getting up. It was not often these days that he had a young man calling round after one of his daughters. Wilfred entered with reluctance. How could he ask Florence to go for a walk with him in front of all these people? He was shown into the parlour by Charity in her wheelchair. She switched the TV on for him.

'Found any good teeth lately?' she teased him.

'None with any gold fillings, but I'm still looking.'

The family reluctantly laid down their playing cards and filed into the front parlour to engage Wilfred in polite conversation and get a good look at him at the same time.

He felt like a fish in a bowl.

Florence sat cursing on the toilet seat. What timing!

'Dad, this is Wilfred,' she said, when she

66

was finally in a position to join them.

'Charity's already done the honours, thanks,' he told her crustily, 'And I must say, you're a sly one, my girl.'

'Oh give over, Dad. It's nothing like that at all. He's a kind friend as promised to take me and Charity up Rivington as soon as it were fine.'

'Tha never told me owt about him.'

'Well I'm telling thee now. Coming, Charity?'

She winked at her aunt.

'What? And miss the rugby? Not likely. But thanks all t'same, Wilfred.'

It was a big sacrifice on Charity's part. Sunshine in the country would have been a great treat. But she knew what was required of her.

However as the door closed on Florrie and Wilfred a cold hand gripped her heart. She imagined the pair of them sharing jokes she could not share and walking through places she could not readily go. She needed Florrie as a child needs its mother. But Florence was not her mother; only her niece. She had a right to a life of her own. Charity felt desolation hovering close.

Old Bill saw the unhappiness in her face.

'We're a right pair of crocks, thee and me,' he said, in an attempt at kindness. He hobbled to the corner cupboard. 'Want a beer?'

'You're a bright spark, Wilfred Robinson,' Florrie reproached him as soon as they were outside.

'How did you know I was going to take you a walk up Rivi?' he asked, stumbling on the kerb in his eagerness to make a good impression by walking on the outside of the pavement.

'I didn't. But I had to get you away from Dad somehow. He'll go on about it now, you'll see. Just like a cat that knows you've got a turkey thawing. No peace.'

'I'm sorry if I've done the wrong thing.'

'Come on.' She took his arm. 'I'm glad you came. Let's enjoy the afternoon.'

And they did.

Lucy's phone rang.

'Have you heard?' came Eileen's voice, heavy with hot news.

'You know me, Eileen. I never hear anything except from you.'

'Well apparently Len Grimshaw hasn't been seen since last Tuesday afternoon?'

'Is there anything unusual in that?'

'Very. He doesn't disappear when he goes on a bender; he just gets found in a heap in the gutter.'

'What about Sheena? She's not in work. What's she going to do?'

'Oh she's moved in with some young feller up the lane. A bad lot by all accounts.

There's only one way she can end up. She's no good, I'm afraid.'

'Be fair, Eileen. What chance has she had?'

'She had a good job at Mrs Bretherton's dress shop. She could have made something of herself.'

'She was useful on baritone,' Lucy affirmed. Then she realised she was speaking in the past tense. 'Is,' she corrected herself.

'I'm going to Chorley with Chantal,' Rebecca shouted up the stairs to her mum, then darted out of the front door and shut it behind her before anybody could ask her what she was going for or express a desire to come too.

Clint Thistleton, the best-looking boy in the fifth form, had asked her to go for a walk with him. Dad had already told her she was too young for boyfriends. Rachel was nearly sixteen and she did not have one. Rachel would go berserk if she knew. The thought of that was more terrifying than merely being sent to her room by Dad.

She met him by the park gates, where he shyly took her hand and they wandered through the park towards the milk bar, neither knowing quite what to say to the other.

They had a milk shake and then wandered down to the canal. They took the bridge to reach the path on the other side and leaned together on the parapet, their heads close.

He pointed to some dark shapes which were moving about in the shadow of the bridge.

'See those?'

'What are they?'

'Trout.'

He was showing off and she was impressed. She could hardly even make them out in the murky water.

'Do you go fishing?'

'Now and again. My dad goes. You have to look in the shady places to see them best.'

Rebecca looked for shady places under the bridge. The water drifted by slowly. It was muddy but she could make out stones and part of an old pram.

'What's that?' she asked. 'Down there where there's a lot of weed. That pale thing.'

'Where?'

'There, just under the bridge. It's shaped like a hand.'

'Oh yes. I see where you mean.' he paused. 'It does look a bit like a hand. Somebody's rubbish. Rubber glove?'

Rebecca stared at it. She felt a shiver go down her spine.

'Let's go back. I'm scared.'

'Scared?' he laughed at her, but kindly. Trust a girl to be scared. 'There's nothing to be scared of. It's just a bit of rubbish. You wait here. I'll go and show you it's nothing.'

So Clint boldly crossed the bridge and climbed down to the water's edge just to prove that the object was not a hand and what he found of course was that it was a hand.

'We've got to report it, Rebecca,' he insisted as he returned, pale of face. 'We can't just go away and leave a body in the water. Just like that.'

'No no. I can't. I can't go to the police. They'll kill me at home. I'm supposed to be in Chorley with Chantal.'

She started to cry, so he walked her back to the lane and made the trip to the police station by himself.

'I've come to report a body,' Clint announced.

The desk sergeant cast a glance at the calendar. April the first was not yet upon them.

'Name?'

'I don't know its name.'

'*Your* name, please.'

'Oh. Clint Thistleton.'

The policeman threw his pencil over his shoulder.

'And my name's Batman. Now off you go sonny or I'll have you for wasting police time.'

'But we – I've just found a body. It's in the canal. Under the bridge. And my name *is* Clint Thistleton,' he added, deeply offended.

Well it had been a boring old day, so the

sergeant sent one of the rookie coppers to accompany Clint to the scene of the crime, if such it should turn out to be, armed with a grappler for dragging ponds with. He gave the young novice orders to watch out for any booby traps at the other end.

The bobby was only a couple of years older than Clint. They remembered one another from school and chattered away about funny things that had happened in the classroom. They filled one another in with what they had been doing since and their plans for the future. On arrival at the canal bridge, Clint showed him the place where he had seen the hand in a clump of weeds, relieved to find that it was still there. The policeman dragged the whole clotted tangle to the edge of the footpath, where, with Clint's help, he was able to pull it ashore.

Then he unclipped the walkie-talkie radio from his belt and called the station.

By Monday morning the next low-pressure system had swept in from the Atlantic with its cargo of rain. Judith and Wendy trudged down Railway Road under a fancy umbrella that did its best, but was hardly up to the task. It was difficult not to walk into people because they could be seen only at the last minute through what looked like a curtain of beads. Cars cast spray over their ankles. The hems of their macs became dripping and muddy, slapping coldly against their calves.

'Run, quick!' ordered Judith as she left Wendy at the gate. Then she hurried on to her own school, hoping Wendy would not have become damp under her gabardine mac.

As she splashed across the playground of the comprehensive, a figure sprang from the car park and dashed towards her.

'Got room for me under that brolly?'

It was Joe Greenhalgh.

The answer should have been 'no', but the question was rhetorical. He crouched under Judith's modest umbrella with his arm around her shoulder and his head close to hers. She could smell his after-shave.

The feel of his hand on her shoulder stayed with her all morning.

'What's this?' Adam poked with his toe the scuffed leather case shaped like a leg of mutton.

'That's Sheena's baritone. I'd lay off if I were you.'

Steve sat straddling the back of a kitchen chair, arms resting along the top. A can of beer was in one hand and a spliff in the other.

'I've always wanted to play one of these things.'

Adam began picking at the clasps.

'She'll have your goolies for golf balls if you touch that thing.'

'Since when did she take up golf?'

Adam got the case open.

'Sheena!' Steve raised his voice above the transistor radio that was on full volume, 'Adam's trying to get into your secret places.'

The sudden silence was as if they had gone deaf. Sheena stood there with one hand hanging in the air, gory with wet nail-varnish, whilst the index finger of the other hand was clamped on the off button of the trannie.

'Leave it alone,' she snapped. 'You couldn't blow the candles out on a two-year-old's...'

She was interrupted by a thunderous knocking at the front door. Adam abandoned the baritone, to peer cautiously through a corner of the window expecting to see the irate form of a neighbour wanting to complain again about the loud music. But it was not a neighbour.

'It's the coppers!'

Both young men sprang into action, grabbing packets from odd corners and heading for the emergency exit that was the back window.

'Answer it slowly, Sheen,' Steve called as they disappeared.

There were two officers on the doorstep, a man and a woman. Why a woman?

'Is your name Sheena Grimshaw?'

Sheena hesitated. How did they know her name?

'Yeah.'

'Can we come in?'

'This isn't my place.'

'We want to talk to you – in private.'

A glance up and down the lane revealed people standing at every doorway, looking in their direction. The police had been hammering at the door for some time.

'All right.'

Sheena stepped aside and let them in. As she followed them down the hall she saw the state of the place through their eyes. It was not a pretty sight. She showed them into what passed for the lounge. But did not invite them to sit down.

'What do you want?' she asked, bluntly.

'Is your father Len Grimshaw?'

'That's not my fault, is it?'

There was an awkward pause.

'Would you like to sit down?' the police-woman put in – quite kindly, it seemed.

'No thanks.'

If she sat, they would sit, then she would never get rid of them.

'When did you see him last?'

'Ages ago. Haven't seen him for ages.'

'When was it, do you remember?'

'It was the day I got the sack. He gave me a beating, so I left. Ask Mrs Bretherton. She can tell you when that was. What's all this about?'

The policeman brought out something from his pocket. It was a silver metal chain with an identity plate on it – such as is worn by epileptics – or alcoholics.

'Do you recognise this?'

Sheena sat down.

'Is he dead?'

'Yes.'

She put her head in her hands, shaking off the hand which the WPC put on her shoulder. She knew exactly what had happened. But she felt nothing. Only relief.

The two officers exchanged glances.

'We'd like you to come with us, when you feel ready,' the policewoman ventured to say.

'I haven't done nothing.'

'I'm afraid we need you to identify the – to identify him.'

'I don't want to. I don't want to see – him.'

'Shall we come back tomorrow?'

They had to get an identification from a close relative. Until then they could not let the world know of his death.

Sheena realised that they would come back when Steve and Adam were here. Steve would not like that. He might throw her out. She forced herself to her feet.

'Oh all right,' she conceded. 'I'll come.'

Casually, as they retraced their steps down the hall, the policeman spoke.

'These blokes you're living with; did you tell them your father beat you up?'

'No no. I didn't tell them. I never said

nothing. They didn't know nothing about it.'

But she could hear her own voice rising hysterically.

'Come along,' said the policewoman gently. 'We've got a car outside.'

The old van with the words *Bill Ainscough's Hot Stompers* peeling off the side chugged and coughed down Babylon Lane and across the busy Ridgeway to the practice room in Railway Road.

'You never told us anything about this feller you're hanging about with, Florence. Is he married, or something?'

That was Gladys, thoroughly jealous.

'Oh he's just one of the regulars at the Spinners. His wife died last year.'

'Losing no time, is he? He wants someone to keep house for him, I expect.'

'Oh shut up, Gladys. You're making too much of it.'

'And concentrate on your driving,' added Alice from behind. 'That number twenty-two bus nearly had us that time.'

'Just remember,' cautioned Florence, 'that this van contains the quality section of Lucy Brindle's band. One false move could ruin the hopes of many handicapped children.'

Gladys said nothing, but turned into the car park, where the ruts in the gateway made them rock like camel-riders.

Lucy was standing at her special conductor's stand as they trundled in through the pub's back door. She had bought it at a recent auction. Now that she had a couple of full scores to read she needed it. It felt good. She did not pretend to be a female Barbirolli, but it made her a real instrumental conductor, however humble. She leafed through the music she had selected for the evening's rehearsal. How soon would she be needing to move on to better pieces? It was not as if they had the current ones off note-perfect. But all of her ladies – as she thought of them – had already known how to play when they had joined her band, so had various levels of competence. It was a matter of getting the lesser lights to shine more brightly; of blending them as an ensemble and not having them just blow as a collection of individuals.

The trick was to find music which would give plenty to those sections which were strong and no tricky bits for the weaker sisters. Since it was unusual to be rich in trombones and poor in cornets this was a problem. She must go through the catalogues and find some trombone speciality numbers.

But new music was expensive. Who was going to pay for it?

She put the arrangement of 'Eventide' on top of the pile as a warmer-upper, after which she would run through 'The Old Castle' and look again at the 'Scottish Airs'.

After the break she would launch a blitz-krieg on 'Regimental Selection', which was not proving as popular as she had hoped.

From all around her came the sounds of people walking in, taking instruments from cases, exchanging greetings and chit-chat. There was the scraping of chairs and the puffing into instruments to warm them up. Florence began her slow lip-slurring exer-cises, working her way patiently up the scale. Judith blew a few restrained long notes and began fiddling about unscrewing the valve casings and dabbing oil on the valves. Rebecca sat down and blew through the scale straight up to a top C which cracked after half a second. Lucy decided it was time she had a word with them all about proper preparation. Harry said that long notes were best for getting the lips in working order.

Most of them did not warm up their lips at all, unless chatting to each other about the price of groceries could be deemed as such.

Looking around, Lucy saw that everybody was there. Even Sheena had arrived on time, though there was something about her that put Lucy in mind of a Persian cat she used to have whose coat would lose its gloss when all was not well.

'I've got a surprise for you.'

Eileen's voice came from behind her shoulder and at that moment in tottered Susie and her brother Philip bearing an E flat bass between them. It was rather a battered old thing, but a sight to gladden the eyes, if not the ears. Lucy thanked Philip as he set off to walk back home up the lane. She smiled a glad welcome at Susie and found her a place next to the bass trombone. They could, she told herself, support one another.

'Let's start with "Eventide".'

There was a riffling of paper before they were ready, mouthpieces poised and holding her gaze. Lucy brought the baton down and the warm blaze of many brass instruments shone upon her. There was some discrepancy in the tuning between Susie and Florence. There was some mistiming between Judith and Annette. But she would sort it all out in time.

It was a noisy break. The younger players had clustered around Susie's bass, taking it in turns to blow. Lucy let them have five minutes, not wanting to discourage their interest, then called them to their places, before it became more than the older ones could bear. She put up 'Regimental Selection'. There were some slippery passages, which she was not sure they could negotiate. But they picked their way along doggedly for the rest of the evening until she took pity on them and sounded the retreat. It was not a good way to finish. Everybody looked a bit depressed. She must bear in mind to finish up with something easy in the future.

There was no motorbike in the shadows when the women trickled out to the car park. Sheena stood hesitant, wondering whether to wait or not.

'Can I give you a lift?' Lucy offered. She was the last to leave. Sheena lived less than a mile up the Lane, but it was steep all the way.

'All right – thanks,' she agreed.

She climbed disconsolately into Lucy's car. The boys must have freaked out without her.

'Are you enjoying the band?' Lucy asked her conversationally, backing out her car.

'Yeah, 's all right.'

Safely in the road, Lucy headed for the crossing to Babylon Lane. 'There's nothing wrong, is there? I thought you were looking a bit down this evening.'

Sheena gave a half laugh.

'Nah.'

'Where do I go from here?' thought Lucy, accelerating across the Ridgeway crossing and out of the path of an articulated lorry which was travelling faster than it should have been.

'They tell me that your father's missing.' she persevered, once in the Lane. 'Has he been found yet?'

'Oh aye.'

'That's good.' Silence. 'I'm really glad to

81

hear it.' The maddening silence continued. 'So is he all right, then?'

'Can you stop just here? That's where I live.'

It was a grim-looking terrace house with a broken window, dripping gutters and nameless gunge around the front step. Sheena hopped out and reached back inside for the baritone.

'He'd been in t'canal a week,' she said in a matter-of-fact tone.

Lucy went hot and cold.

'Oh Sheena. I'm sorry.'

''S all right.'

When she got home Lucy was about to seek sympathy from Harry for her latest trauma, then stopped herself. He would only tell her that she had taken on this task willingly, with all that it entailed and if she did not like the heat she must leave the kitchen. He would have been right, of course.

Chapter 6

The clocks were put forward, everybody missed an hour's sleep and March became April.

One Friday Joe Greenhalgh sought out

Judith in the staff room.

'Are you coming to sit in on wind band after school?'

Judith coloured a little.

'I haven't got my cornet.'

'We can find you one.'

'Perhaps if I just come along and listen this time?'

'You can do that whenever you like.' He gave her a warm smile. 'But don't be too critical, will you?'

'I wouldn't dream of it.'

They sat themselves down together in a remote corner of the staff room and discussed the problems of repertoire and absenteeism and the latest Government White Paper on Education. He said he liked her dress and the bell went and they had to separate.

Judith got through the rest of the lessons in a daze. Why had she said she would like to listen? The sound of the wind band could be even more excruciating than that of form four doing the 'Hallelujah Chorus' on a bad day. How could she be so silly? She was thirty-three and much too old for crushes.

But she went, just the same.

She sat near the back of the hall and watched him conducting. Sunlight came through the side window and caught the hairs on his forearm. His sleeves were rolled up and she could see the muscles working above his wrists. The movement with which he brought in the flutes and clarinets was incredibly graceful. He used his face a good deal and at one point he helped the French horns make a difficult entry with a lift of his eyebrows.

Once, he called across to consult her on a matter of balance and every child turned its face towards her. In spite of her embarrassment, she gave a helpful reply. Afterwards, she tried to slip out quietly, but he caught up with her in the corridor.

'Time for a coffee or something?'

Oh the agony of having to refuse!

'My daughter will wonder where I am. She's only nine.'

'Phone her. She can answer the phone, can't she?'

When he dropped her off at her front door an hour later, she looked ten years younger. Wendy, who had been a little worried, in spite of the phone call, because her mother *never* went anywhere without her, ran to open the front door. She could see at once there was something strange. Judith looked happy.

'Can I come too next time?' she asked wistfully.

Lucy drove to the practice. She was beginning to feel more and more optimistic about

84

the chances of the band. Their numbers were increasing. It was true they still needed more players, but until such could be found, the present ones had good potential. She was lucky there were no total duffers to deal with, though Rachel was a bit lazy and Sheena unreliable. It was a case of bringing everybody to work as a team.

The trombone sisters were already there, as usual. The three of them were now setting out chairs in the required order, shouting unheeded advice across to one another as they did so.

Lucy put her music down on the conductor's stand, which had already been placed out, and glanced through her music, wondering what to concentrate on this evening. To tax the players without disheartening them – that was the way to do it. Absorbed in such matters, she heard a cough at her elbow and turned to find Florence standing there nervously.

Florence – nervous?

'I want you to know, Lucy,' she spoke with uncharacteristic softness, 'that I'm going to be married.'

'Married, Florence?'

I mustn't look thunderstruck, thought Lucy. I mustn't look thunderstruck.

'In July.'

'That's marvellous, Florence. That's splendid news. Congratulations.'

'He's a widower. He's called Wilfred Robinson.'

Lucy heard the warm glow in Florence's voice and was touched.

'It doesn't mean you'll be leaving us, does it?'

'No fear! This band is the best thing that's happened around here since Frederick's ice cream. This band and Wilfred,' she added hastily.

'And you're very important to us. We couldn't carry on without you. I know we've got a bass now, but Susie isn't ready to carry the sound on her own. Please give her all the help you can.'

'Best thing you could do, Lucy, would be to tune us all up before we start. If you tune everybody, then nobody need feel singled out, will they?'

'Thanks for the tip.'

The room was filling up already. Rachel and Rebecca Hetherington had arrived and so had second tenor horn Winifred. Judith and Wendy came through the door. Who would have thought, Lucy mused, that playing top cornet in a band could have brought so much spring into Judith's step, so much light to her eye!

'I wanted to ask you,' continued Florence, who was still hovering beside her, full of the rest of what she had to say, 'if the band would play at our wedding. I know the band hasn't been together long and you weren't planning to go public yet, but it need only be for hymns, and perhaps a march before and after the ceremony. I'd like Mary to play "The Lost Chord" while we're signing the register. It's Wilfred's favourite. There will be an organ in the church, of course, but the band would be more special. And that's what I'd like – what we'd like. Wilfred wants it too. If it could be managed, of course.'

'Well,' exclaimed Lucy, a little over-whelmed by the length of the speech as much as by its content. 'I feel honoured to be asked. We'll have to see if everybody can make it.'

Once everybody had arrived, unpacked her instrument and put up her music stand, Lucy waited until they had settled and then asked all the B flat instruments to blow a C. The result brought home to her the wisdom of Florence's suggestion.

Taking the lead from Annette's trumpet, which was in good tune and the most penetrating in timbre, she prevailed upon each one in turn to coax her C into some kind of similarity. Rachel was flat and Gladys just a fraction sharp. The others were close enough.

But it was when she turned her attention to the E flat instruments that the serious problem emerged. Eileen and Winifred quickly adjusted their Gs, the equivalent note on tenor horns, but Susie was so far out that the room erupted into spontaneous laughter. Luckily Susie was used to being laughed at and contrived to play the same note an octave down just to set them off again. It was all of a semitone sharp.

'Pull out your tuning slide,' suggested Florence. Susie did. It came off in her hand. Wendy, Rachel and Rebecca were in fits of laughter. Even Sheena managed a smile.

Lucy surveyed her flock. To whom could she turn for help?

'Give it to me,' offered Winifred, the pilot's widow. She succeeded in replacing the slide and pulling it out a little, but not nearly as much as it needed to be if the notes were to come out in tune.

'It's the instrument,' opined Florrie, fondly flexing the slide of her good trombone. She knew what a difference it could make. She had been stuck for years on her sub-standard G-bass trombone.

'By the look of it I'd guess it's quite old,' volunteered Winifred. 'I've met some of those in my time. They used to make them in high pitch, you know,' she added. 'Before it was standardised. They called it "continental pitch".'

'That's news to me.'

It was news to most people in the room, and bad news at that.

'What could the school have been thinking

of?' complained Eileen. 'Not to get something done about it.'

'Don't suppose anybody noticed.'

'They're all out of tune, anyway,' contributed Rachel.

'Well can you get anything done about it?' Lucy wanted to know.

'Not without taking it to a metalworker and getting extra length put in,' Winifred told her. 'It's not that expensive, but it's never quite as good as a new one.'

Lucy shook her head and picked up her baton. 'Just pull all the tuning slides out as far as you dare and lip it down as much as you can, Susie.'

That was unlikely to get results. But it would have to do for now.

During the break Mary came and asked Lucy if she could try the cadenza in the 'Medley of Scottish Airs'. She had worked on it at home, to William's delight, and felt she could manage it, though not perhaps at the speed intended.

It looked safe enough. A glance at the score told Lucy that the horn section was holding a chord and the rest of the band was silent. So she put that music on top of her pile and called everybody to their places.

'We're going to do the "Scottish Airs",' she told them. 'Miss out the first pause like you've always done, but when you get to the second one, everybody who's got a note –

play it softly. Mary's going to do the cadenza. Do you want to stand up, Mary?'

'It's just a cadenza, not a recitation.'

So off they went and it sounded quite good, though again there were some untidy entries in the top part, which she began to realise was Annette and not Judith. She stopped them and made them enter again and again until it was neat and tidy.

When they came to Mary's bit, she waved silent the cornets and trombones and left Mary to get on with it. Mary started confidently and rattled up to the top note, but she threatened to stumble on her way down and slowed considerably, like someone negotiating some slippery steps.

This of course put a strain on the three who were holding on to their notes until she finished. Eileen was going scarlet. Winifred gave up. Then there was a crash and Sheena collapsed onto the floor, sending her music stand flying. It knocked over Eileen's and Winifred's and nearly set up a domino effect among the cornets.

Mary put her euphonium down and knelt to turn Sheena over with great gentleness. It was not a fit. She could see that.

'She's fainted.'

'Give her some air.'

'That child is ill,' said Winifred. 'She needs a doctor.'

'She needs a mother.'

Don't we all, thought Lucy, sighing.

'All right, carry her over to those chairs, two of you,' she said aloud. 'You'd better loosen that belt. Susie, will you get some water?'

'What in?'

'Anything you can find.'

'There's some cups in that cupboard by the door,' Eileen told her.

They brought her round and after she'd been helped to the loo to throw up a little, she was able to sit out the rest of the practice looking grey and ghastly. At one point she stood up and started to leave, but Lucy ordered her firmly to sit down again.

Sheena did so. She put her head in her hands. She felt too awful to be rebellious.

Lucy drove her up the Lane afterwards and stopped her car outside the house where the paint peeled and there was dry rot in the window frame. Cardboard failed to cover the broken pane and the front doorknob was missing. She wanted to help but not to interfere. What was the best approach?

'I'll come in and get you a hot drink if you like.'

'No ta. I'll be all right.'

'You must phone a doctor.'

Sheena climbed out shakily.

'I don't need a doctor. I'm not pregnant, Mrs B,' she added, realising that this was almost certainly the thought in every mind now.

'Even so...' Lucy leaned out of her window, wondering how someone of her age could be so sure. 'You're obviously not well, Sheena. Would you like me to phone one for you? I can take you to the surgery if you'd rather make an appointment.'

She might not want a doctor to come visiting that house.

Sheena reached back inside the car for the baritone, which was on the back seat.

'No. 'S all right. Honest.'

'Sheena,' Lucy grabbed her wrist and held on. 'Promise me you'll phone the doctor.'

'Oh all right. I'll phone for a doctor.'

Lucy let go.

'You'll phone tonight.'

'I'll phone tonight.'

Anything to get rid of her.

Sheena swayed up the step, keeping her balance with the aid of the baritone.

Steve would kill her if she phoned for a doctor.

Mary swung William off the step of the bus and landed him at the feet of Alice, who was waiting for them on the platform of Chorley bus station. Then they each took one of his hands and let him do big jumps as they walked along. It was tiring. He was really too heavy for them now, but they had not the heart to tell him so.

When they stopped at the kerb he tugged

at her hand in the direction of Tessa's Tea Rooms, so they went and bought him a Mars Bar and had themselves cups of tea.

'I'm sure it could make a big difference to him if he had special outings like other children,' said Mary, staring out of the window at all the ordinary people for whom shopping and catching a bus was not a problem. 'Billy's quite capable of learning. It's surprising what he can do if you spend some patience on him.'

'That's true.'

'He notices that he gets treated differently from other children. He's quite capable of feeling hurt, too.'

'I know he is,' Alice reassured her gently. She smiled affectionately at her nephew. She thought the world of him. 'I tell you what. Let's go home and see if Dad's got Alf round again this aft.'

'Tease him about his band, you mean.'

'Why not?'

'Want to go and see Aunty Charrers, William?'

'Yush!'

He nodded vigorously.

'There you are. He spoke.'

'He said yes. Say it again, William.'

'Yush.'

They hugged him and left the tea room. Outside they noticed that it was not so cold as it had been.

Lucy and Harry and Eileen and Tom were gracing the lounge bar of the Jumping Trout pub and restaurant, nursing their pre-prandial aperitifs when Lucy broke the news about Florence and Wilfred.

'I hope he knows what he's taking on, poor fellow.'

That was the reaction of Harry.

'I do think you could find something a bit nicer than that to say,' Lucy reproached him.

'We're all invited,' added Eileen. 'All the band. Husbands and boyfriends too.'

'So are you going to take a husband and a boyfriend?' Harry teased her.

'Don't put ideas into her head,' Lucy chided him.

'What's Florrie going to do, then?' Tom wanted to know. 'Add the oompahs from the altar?'

'Don't be daft!'

Eileen pretended to hit him on the head with the rolled-up menu.

'Mary's going to play "The Lost Chord" on the euphonium,' Lucy told them. 'At Wilfred's request. While they're signing the register. Should sound rather nice, I think.'

'What's Wilfred want the lost chord for?' piped up Tom and both men together chorused: 'To keep his pyjama trousers up, of course.'

That kept the pair of them in hoots for half a minute. Lucy sat straight-faced surveying the gleaming vista of metal fillings and meditating on the boy within the man.

'I think it would be better if you two just come to the reception, not the service,' she said.

'I want to hear your band, love,' protested Harry. 'I've never heard you play yet.'

'You can come to t'next practice, if you're that keen.'

That wiped the smiles off their faces.

'Not if I have anything to do with it,' murmured Eileen.

'Only the thing is...' Lucy persevered, 'this is Florrie's special day. It's the one day of her life when she can be the belle of the ball, so to speak.'

'Aye, she'll be t'biggest bell in t'clock tower, our Florrie.'

'There you go, you see. Still laughing at her. I know she's always prepared to laugh at herself, but inside she's quite sensitive. I'm sure of it.'

'Surely you don't think we're going to be cracking jokes in church?'

'Why not? You can't stop cracking them now. It's a tricky job, conducting. I want to keep my mind on it. I'm going to be nervous enough as it is. How can I concentrate if I'm listening for sniggers from the back of the church all the time?'

'All right. If that's what you want.'

'Well surely you can see it's for the best.'

'As long as we're allowed in at the reception,' put in Tom. He was not mad about church services anyway. The reception was the bit that mattered as far as he was concerned.

They were called to their table and seated themselves. The men began to discuss the current demand for pay rises in the pit, so the conversation of Lucy and Eileen turned, as it often did these days, to the band.

'I was wondering whether to offer to take Sheena to practices and bring her back every Wednesday. Then at least she won't be late.'

Lucy lobbed the idea across to Eileen.

'If you think it's worth it,' Eileen said dubiously. 'I'm not sure we wouldn't be better off without that girl. She could give us all a bad name.'

'I wish we could get her away from that boy she's with. I'm sure he's a bad influence. Do you think he's encouraging her to take drugs?'

'I'm sure he is. But does she need much encouraging?'

'Probably not. I suppose he's all she's got. I suppose she hasn't anywhere else to go now.'

'Don't interfere, Lucy. He's dangerous. They say he's capable of anything. What I can't understand is why she wants to keep coming to band. Not exactly her scene, is it?'

'I wonder if it isn't some kind of cry for help,' mused Lucy. 'She's not working any more. She has no family. We're her only contact with normal life. Does she perhaps not want to lose her contact with normal life?'

'Normal life!' exclaimed Tom, overhearing. 'If women playing brass instruments is normal life, my name's Harry Mortimer.'

'Pleased to meet you,' snapped Lucy.

'Don't ask me if it's a cry for help or not. I'm not a psychiatrist,' put in Eileen, having waited with her mouth open ready to speak as if Tom had not interrupted. 'And none of us is going to get that close to her. Nobody else is her age. I can't see Rachel befriending her – not with that straight-laced background.'

'I take it you and Tom don't get on with next door but one.'

'It's nothing. A big fuss about nothing.'

'Tell me about this nothing. I'm intrigued.'

'There's nothing to be intrigued about.'

She would say no more, which of course left Lucy doubly intrigued.

Chapter 7

Easter came and went. The evenings grew lighter and the weather was inclement less often. The women continued to meet regularly, becoming more familiar with the pieces all the time, though it was a slow process. They also got to know one another better, because of all the chatting that took place whenever there was a break from playing. The collection of individuals was slowly blending into one unit.

Lucy noticed more changes in Judith. The severe hairdo she used to sport, with everything pulled back into a tight bun, disappeared. In its place was a fashionable trim. Her dresses were brighter in colour. She held herself more erect and smiled more. There was a liveliness about her face that made her seem much younger.

'You do look festive,' Lucy could not help remarking one Wednesday, when she turned up wearing earrings.

It was beginning to show at school, too. The pupils, always quick to see liaisons between members of the staff, even when they did not exist, were already pairing off Judith and Mr Greenhalgh in the bicycle-shed gossip.

In any case, it was the season for romance, as Shakespeare has been quick to point out. But Judith's fancy had not turned to thoughts of love for many a long spring.

As the weather improved she would take Wendy for weekend walks. Now suddenly she noticed how all around them the world of nature was opening up. The leaves were green and tender. The hedgerows grew vivid with bluebells. Like overflowing bowls of cream the hawthorn blossoms hung, filling the air with the scent of approaching summer. The heavens were balmy with birdsong. All good things were on their way.

Her heart was like a frozen limb thawing in the rays of the sun. The life was flowing back into it. But the pain, when it came, was going to be bad. On Tuesday morning he had passed her in the corridor without speaking and she felt as if she had been kicked by a horse. That should have been enough warning for her. Stop now before it gets worse. Get out. Write him off.

Then as she sat picking over her dinner in a corner of the refectory she had looked up to see him standing beside her with two cups of tea. She pulled out the chair next to hers as if it were the most natural thing. Her heartache vanished. He sat down and asked her how the morning's lessons had gone and told her about a funny thing which had happened among the oboes. She laughed and he laughed. Then she asked his advice about the kind of songs which might appeal to fifth formers. All too soon the dinner break was over and they had to go their separate ways.

Treading air all the way to the music room, she knew she was lost.

But she no longer dreaded school.

On Wednesday evening the setting sun burst out from below a belt of clouds in a blaze of crimson as Lucy drove into the car park at the Spinners Arms. A sign of glories to come, she told herself, knowing it was more likely to mean blood, sweat and tears. As usual the Ainscough sisters had put the chairs out and were assembling their trombones. But Florence came and made a beeline for her. She strode forwards purposefully, hands behind her back. Then, as though giving a child a birthday present, she whipped out one hand and placed a large envelope on Lucy's stand. She watched, beaming, as Lucy extracted the contents. It was a set of parts and a conductor's copy for a piece called 'Tightrope Walker'. Underneath the title were the words 'Trombone Solo'.

'That's a gift because you're playing at our wedding,' she told Lucy. 'I thought you might want it now.'

'Better not change your mind at the last minute, then,' Lucy teased her, 'or we'll have to give it back.'

'No danger of that,' protested Florence, taking the joke quite seriously.

Lucy opened the score and glanced through it. It was exactly what she wanted; or almost, since it featured first trombone and not all three of them. Excitedly, she took it across to Alice who, it turned out, had not been informed.

'You might have said something to me about it first,' complained Alice to her sister. 'You might have consulted me. You'll have to play it yourself.'

Florrie's face fell. She would love to have been given such a chance to shine.

'I thought you'd be pleased.'

But Alice did not share her extrovert nature.

'It's written for tenor trombone,' Lucy pointed out. 'That's a different clef from your bass. Would Gladys take it on?'

'No,' came the flat answer from Gladys, who had been observing the scene from a safe distance.

'I can read treble,' Florence told her.

'Won't it be too high?'

'I can play high notes. When I practise them.'

'Are you in practice now?'

'Sort of.'

'Put the parts out, then. You can show me the high notes as and when they occur.'

And she did. She was superb.

She had actually run through the piece several times already, first to see if it was OK for Alice, then because she liked it; then because she could not leave it alone. She realised she should have let Alice see it, but had selfishly kept it to herself so that she could enjoy it to the full before handing it over. Now she knew it well enough to milk all the opportunities for humour in the bits where she was unaccompanied. Lucy realised she had a show-stopper on her hands.

But all was not well with the cornets.

She waited until the half-time break, then she took Judith aside.

'How's Annette getting along?'

'She's a great support. I'm glad to have her there.'

'Any problems?'

'Not as long as she knows the tune.'

'And she didn't know the tune we've just played.'

'She can sight-read to some extent. It's her timing. I think – the thing is – some of her playing is really good. She's got a technique like she's been really well taught.'

'What is it, then?' Lucy saw Annette watching from the corner of her eye, so she lowered her voice still further and turned her back.

'I don't think she'd ever seen a rest before she came to us. I reckon she must have practised by herself and played solos all the time and – well – she can't count. That's what it boils down to. She never knows where to come in. If she waits for me she comes in slightly behind and if she doesn't she comes in too soon.'

'I suppose that's what makes the difference playing in a band – to playing by yourself, I mean. What should I do about it? Have a word with her?'

'No. Better not to offend her. Give her time. I'm sure she'll get the knack in time. It's just a question of getting used to waiting for your turn. I like having her there. She's not afraid to play out. She's got much more confidence than I have. It would be a pity to take it away – her confidence, I mean. It's hard to get it back once it's gone.'

There speaks one who knows, thought Lucy.

'Thanks for your advice,' she said aloud. 'I'll leave it then.'

Judith turned away.

'Oh and – I like your hair like that,' Lucy added, thinking to bolster Judith's growing self-confidence, since the subject had been raised. 'It makes you look younger.'

'Thank you,' said Judith, going pink.

The Whitsun weekend was a scorcher. Those who had cars made for Southport or Blackpool. Those who did not took to the parks and the countryside.

Judith took Wendy for a walk as far as the Upper Reservoir. Wendy loved the countryside. There was always something to look at. There were trees to identify and birds and hundreds of different wild flowers about the place. She would pounce eagle-eyed on any she did not recognise and ask for their names. If her mother did not know, and she frequently did not, Wendy would write a description and a sketch of the foliage in her little notebook so that she could check when she went back to school.

She stopped by a section of pale stone wall where little tufts of grass grew bravely in the mortar. A bird had flown into one of the cavities as they approached and, squinting inwards, Wendy's eye was met by the round yellow gaze of a female blackbird, frightened, but keeping guard. There was a cheeping sound.

'Mummy! There's some baby birds in here.'

Attracted by her cries, a large black Labrador dog bounded up and began to bark, pawing at the loose stones and threatening to dislodge them.

'Go away!' Wendy shouted, throwing a stick at it.

Of course, it ran after the stick quite happily, picked it up and brought it back to her, wagging its tail.

'Mummy, make it go away.'

But Mummy was not paying attention. She was watching the dog's owner as he came up to them. It was Mr Greenhalgh. Wendy's day was immediately ruined. When he was around, her mother was a different person.

'Oxo! Come here. Good boy. Heel!' he called. The dog hesitated, then reluctantly went to his master to have his ears rubbed. Mr Greenhalgh assured Wendy it was quite friendly, which was more than could be said for Wendy. She tagged along grumpily, dragging her feet as they walked past the reservoir, admiring the view. She gave the dog a surreptitious slap on the hind quarters to make it clear to the animal that it would have no favours from her. She and it were consigned to the sidelines from now on. It was not a nice feeling to be relegated like that when she and her mum had been each other's close companions for so long.

She trailed along behind them through the lanes and round the reservoir sulking all the way and scarcely managed to be gracious even when he bought her an ice cream. It only increased the attention the stupidly named dog was giving her.

Then with incredible swiftness, the sky darkened and before they could return home a thunderstorm broke around them. They all found shelter under the archway of a stone gate and huddled together. He had his arm around her mother and she giggled in a silly way. Oxo's wet tail kept hitting Wendy's legs.

It was this same thunderstorm that was the undoing of Sheena's boyfriend Steve and his sidekick Adam. They had noticed half the population leaving for the open spaces and were quickly off to do a tour of the empty houses to see what they could pick up. But they found a full liquor cabinet and failed to notice that the weather had changed. They lost track of the time, or of the number of bottles consumed.

The unfortunate householder who came back too soon was clubbed down while his family looked on. But the wife gave such a good description of the pair that the local police knew who it was at once.

All they had to do was call round quickly enough to catch them while they were still groggy with booze.

When Sheena saw the boys being over-powered she went berserk and kicked and bit the officers. It took three of them to restrain her. So of course she had to be taken away and charged as well.

So the following Wednesday Lucy made a virtue of necessity by working on the pieces which the band would have to be playing at the wedding. She brought out arrangements she had borrowed from various sources for *Crimond* and Handel's *Largo*, as well as Sullivan's 'The Lost Chord', with a solo part for the euphonium.

She was glad that she could turn the band's attention to hymns while their baritone was missing. With hymns all the instrumental resources were concentrated into four parts, so that the baritone role was well and truly covered by the euphonium and by Gladys on second trombone.

Against the odds, the sound was quite good. All the tunes were familiar, which was a great help. Annette could play *Crimond* and its ilk boldly, without having to count.

Lucy had her little speech ready for the half-time break. She reminded them about the wedding, which was approaching at a rate of knots. She told them how pleased she was that they were all going to be available. She urged them to play their best to make it an occasion of which Florrie and Wilfred could be proud, since they had been kind enough to invite everyone – husbands as well, those that have them – to the reception.

Then she paused, took a breath and panned their faces.

'I expect you've all heard the sad news about Sheena.' Another pause. 'At the moment she's remanded in custody pending further enquiries and a probationer's report.

I'm a little concerned, because she has no close relatives at all who will be in a position to visit her, and no friends who might feel inclined to either.

'If there is anybody here who is prepared to go and see her at the prison, I'll organise a rota, so that we can spread ourselves over the time that she's there and she needn't feel people have forgotten her. Hands up any volunteers.'

The hands of Eileen and Florence flew up at once, followed by Winifred, Mary and – surprisingly – Annette. Judith held back. The idea repelled her. She would not know what to say. It repelled Alice, too, but she put up a tentative hand just the same. Rachel and Rebecca said they would have to ask their dad. Susie put her hand up and was made to put it down again sharpish by Eileen. Twelve was too young.

'Do you think it's a good idea, Lucy?' Gladys felt that somebody had to speak up in the respectability lobby. 'What sort of image is it going to give the band if we're all trotting off to the prison every five minutes?'

'I'm not sure if it's a good idea or not,' Lucy replied crushingly. 'But it's something I think we ought to do just the same.'

Gladys did not feel she could argue with that, failing any support from the others. But neither did she volunteer. Appearances were made to be kept up, in her view.

They dispersed for their break. Annette stayed where she was, passing the time by taking a soft cloth and giving the trumpet's bell an unnecessary polish. Beside her Judith was scanning through a page of music, humming to herself.

'You're looking very glam these days,' Annette felt driven to remark. 'Found a new hairdresser?'

'It's that Mr Greenhalgh,' came Wendy's truculent tones from behind. She saw much less of her mother these days. HE would bring her back from school in his car and sometimes she would be ages out there in the road chatting.

'Where's his salon?' Annette wanted to know. 'He's a new one on me.'

'He's not a hairdresser,' Wendy told her, in a voice that made her feelings on the matter unmistakable. 'He's a teacher.'

'Oh really? Tell me more.'

Annette's voice dripped with curiosity.

'That's enough, Wendy,' Judith told her pinkly. 'You know what children are,' she added to Annette.

'I should do,' said Annette. 'I've got three of them.'

'Oh really? How did you manage to stay so slim?' asked Judith, successfully turning the conversation away from herself.

'I work at it,' Annette told her. 'Exercises. It doesn't just happen. I take the dogs for a walk every day, rain or shine and eat the right things...'

Judith listened politely, but her mind was already drifting back to that which haunted her waking hours and tantalised her sleep. Joe was taking more and more opportunities to see her, though without committing himself to the steady relationship she so longed for.

'I'm afraid I'll be getting you talked about,' Judith had dared to suggest, though rather belatedly, when he had dropped her off home.

'Yes you will,' he agreed. 'How about making it an evening next time? Give the tongues something to wag about.'

He wiggled his eyebrows at her. Judith was speechless. 'See you,' he grinned and drove away with a boyish vroom of the engine.

Chapter 8

The days grew longer. The band worked on below strength. However, such players as there were began to cohere quite nicely. Another advertisement was placed, this time in the *Horwich Journal*, asking for more players, and a couple of young mums called Joan and Deirdre turned up. They were friends and played cornets, but could not be regular or reliable because they had very young families. Never mind. Lucy was still pleased to have them, if only as part-timers. Cornets were needed more desperately than anything else. She would have preferred to have them at the practice every week, since they were both capable of taking a top line, but if they could attend a few rehearsals and be there both for the concert and the festival it would be an enormous help.

But even as the cornets were strengthened, the horn section was weakened without the baritone.

Meanwhile, Sheena's day was again brightened with the message:

'Grimshaw, you've got a visitor.'

Her spirits rose. Who would it be this time? Lucy had been to see her. And Eileen. And Winifred. She had never expected to have any visitors at all. Now so many were turning up that her cell-mate was getting quite jealous. The warders were beginning to treat her with a grudging respect. Who would it be today? she wondered. It made all the difference to her dreary routine to know that she would have someone from 'outside' to talk to. However, when she saw Annette waiting on the other side of the divide she had to admit that it was not the first person she would have chosen. She was tempted to turn and walk back to her cell. Yet Lucy was right. Any face was better than none. If Annette started acting all superior she could always give her an earful. Sheena was good at giving people earfuls.

'Hi,' Annette greeted her languidly.

She handed Sheena a jar of pink bath salts.

Sheena turned it round, looking carefully at the contents, as the supervisor regarded them both with narrowed eyes.

'Anything in it?' Sheena asked mischievously.

'No files. No drugs. No map of the premises, if that's what you mean.'

'Thanks, anyway.'

Annette sighed inwardly. She felt sorry for Sheena, but had not expected to have met with such truculence.

'What's it like in there, then?' she asked, in an effort to get some kind of conversation going. 'Bread and water? Or fish and chips?'

'Proper home from home. What did you think?'

Annette stared at the shiny eau-de-nil walls, running with condensation. The windows were high and small and barred. The furniture rudimentary.

She thought about her lounge at home, with its full-length velvet curtains flanking the French windows and the view over lawn and flower beds to the reservoir beyond. She thought of the Axminster carpets, the G-Plan furniture, the Rowland Hilder prints on the walls.

'Got a lawyer?' she asked.

'They sent this berk round. Won't let me see Steve.'

To her annoyance, Sheena felt her lip tremble.

'You'll see him at the trial.'

'Yeah. Between two coppers. Be able to wave to him from the other side of the room, maybe. Big thrill!'

She chewed at her lip. Crying in front of Lucy would have been bad enough – but in front of Madame Fashion House...!

'When's that going to be?'

'Don't ask me.' She swallowed. 'Christmas, at this rate.'

'That's not good enough, Sheena. We need our baritone. I guess we'll have to get the girls together and spring you.'

Sheena dropped her head. She gave a little snort of laughter.

'Them trombone cases'd hold a shotgun or two,' she observed.

Annette giggled.

'Keep the engine running, Gladys...'

'If you can...'

They both became consumed with laughter and Sheena was glad to pull out a tissue and mop her eyes.

The supervisor looked on bemused.

Sheena had never been seen even to smile before.

The sands of June were running out and for once Judith was not looking forward to the end of term. Would he want to see her in the holidays? If not, how would she survive for six weeks without him? He had taken her out to the pictures twice and once to a football match, with Wendy, who had sulked all the way through it. But he avoided making an ongoing commitment. At first she had intended to get Mavis to find out if he was married, but now she held back. People of her persuasion did not make dates with married men.

He had never mentioned a wife, but he was too old to be single and normal. He must be widowed or divorced, she told herself. He had to be. Any other thought she refused to entertain.

At the mid-morning break on one of the last Fridays of the term, he came over to where she was chatting to Mavis Fielding and put his hand on her shoulder. She tingled from head to foot.

'I've had to cancel wind band today.'
'Oh really?'
'Yes, because of the exams.'
'Of course. The exams.'
'I thought I ought to let you know.'
'That was very kind of you.'

114

'In case you were going to stay and listen again.'

'I expect I would have done. If you hadn't told me.'

The words were of the stuff of ditch water. But the conversation they were having with their eyes was pretty exciting.

Then the English master came up and started a discussion about the end-of-term concert, puffing pipe smoke over the four of them. Judith listened and nodded and smiled in the right places, but she was conscious only of the fact that Joe's elbow kept brushing her arm.

The bell went and Mavis winked at her.

'I must fly. I've got the first form on the tennis courts, so help me, learning to serve.'

'We'll give you a good funeral,' quipped the English master.

'Thanks a lot.'

He waved his pipe at her, but made no move to depart. He had a free period and could outlast them all. She could tell by the way Joe made his farewell that he had been hoping to have a word in private. So Judith turned away with a feeling of opportunity lost. However, at dinner time she found a note in her pigeon hole.

'There is a matter I must discuss with you,' it read. *'Can I pick you up at eight o'clock tonight? J.G.*

PS – get a babysitter.'

Alice's turn to visit Sheena finally came. It had to be undergone! She put on her best coat and her smartest shoes and took the bus from the Ridgeway. She had never been to a prison before and wanted to look as respectable as she could, which was a good reason for leaving the van at home. Of going into the place she was confident. It was the coming out again she wanted to be sure of.

Nervously, she arrived at the appointed hour and rang the bell. The door swung open heavily and a stern-looking person let her in. The place gave her the creeps. Fancy being shut in here for you did not know how long! Poor Sheena!

She had brought along a couple of *True Romances*, because she understood there was not much to read in prisons except Ancient Tomes, whatever they were. They sounded dusty and boring anyway. But *True Romances* helped her pass her own time in a most agreeable fashion.

'There's a lot more where those came from, if you like that kind of thing, Sheena. Just say the word.'

'Thanks a lot, Alice. You're a pal.'

Though she never allowed her hard-boiled façade to falter, Sheena was in fact deeply moved by the attention she was receiving from the band. She would be the first to spit in the eye of anyone who condescended to

116

her. But none of them had. Not even Annette. They had cared enough to come and see her and to bring the kind of thing which they themselves would like to have been given; fashion mags from Eileen, bath salts from Annette, comics from Rachel, and from Florrie a calendar with a fresh joke for every day, to cheer her up and help count the time to her release.

She had never had so many presents in her life before. 'Chief Hood wants to see you before you go,' she told her visitor.

'Chief Hood?' Alice went pale with alarm.

'The Governor, to you. It's like as not to tell you something to pass on to Mrs Brindle. Perhaps you'd like to tell me, when she's told you, 'cos I'm interested too.'

It was unwelcome news for Alice. Why could she not have chosen somebody else's visiting day? She was so worried about it that she could not concentrate on chatty gossip and made a totally unsatisfactory visitor.

She had to wait outside the Governor's door. It was a long time since she had been at school, but it brought back to her as though the intervening years were nothing those awful visits to the headmistress's study. The door was old panelled wood, just the same. The corridor echoed and there were sounds of distant voices and door-slams and the smell of disinfectant, just like school.

At last she was invited to go in.

'Do sit down.'

Alice sat.

'I gather you're not related to the remand prisoner Grimshaw.'

'Just a friend.'

'We want to find, if possible, someone to be *in loco parentis*.'

'Come again?'

'Her trial will be soon. There may be more serious charges made, or again there may not. She may get a suspended sentence. The Probation Office has been asking whether there is a responsible adult she could go to in that event.'

'None that I know of.'

'That's a pity.'

Alice thought for a minute, before deciding to pass the buck in its usual direction.

'I think you'd better talk to Mrs Brindle.'

Judith was ready long before eight. She had arranged for Wendy to have a sleep-over at a school friend's house. There would be no need to hurry home. The sound of Joe's car arriving set her heart beating. She grabbed her jacket and handbag and flew outside to meet him. He installed her in the passenger seat of his white sports car and whisked her over the moors to a pub in Darwen; far from the risk of a chance encounter with any of their pupils.

'What'll you have?' he asked as he found

her a seat in the rear courtyard, where a climbing rose spread its perfume over them.

'Orange juice, please.'

'What with?'

'Just orange juice.'

'You can't just have orange juice.'

'I'm Salvation Army,' Judith told him, feeling as though she were making a thoroughly damning confession – which, in his view, she was. She saw his face fall and a shadow was cast on her evening.

'Don't you ever have alcohol?' he asked in the tone in which he would ask a blind man if he had never seen the sea.

'I've had a sherry, at Christmas – sometimes.'

Twice, if the truth were known.

'Good,' he said. 'Sweet or dry?'

'Sweet.'

He disappeared, while she brought out her mirror to check her hair was still in place and agonised as to whether she had just killed off a beautiful relationship. Then he reappeared with her sherry and a whisky for himself and all was well again.

'What was it you wanted to discuss with me.'

'Nothing, really. I just wanted an excuse to get you to myself.'

'You don't need an excuse for that, you know.'

'I know.' Their eyes met. For a few minutes

there was nothing to say.

Finally he broke the silence.

'Actually, I wondered what you're doing this summer. You going away at all?'

'I haven't made any plans.'

'I'm taking the school band to the Lake District for the August bank holiday week-end. I could do with another member of staff to help with the kids. Female, if possible.'

Judith's mouth fell open a little. Her heart beat fast.

'Drink up,' he said. 'I'll get you another one.'

'No really...'

But he went and got them each another one and of course she could not waste it. Two was all Judith needed for the effects to begin to tell. She felt wicked, but happy, seized by an unfamiliar euphoria.

He drove her to the moors to watch the sunset. She leaned towards him, longing to put her head on his shoulder. He put his arm around her and drove with one hand on the steering wheel. It felt wonderful to be driven thus, to be part of a couple. She could not be sure he was her man, but he felt like her man. It was a good feeling. The heavy arm around her shoulders made her feel shaky with desire. She could remember what it felt like to have a man's lips on hers, a man's chin against her face.

Was he free? She had not asked when she

could have and now it was not wise. She had been brought up to strict rules which it was better to break unknowingly if you were going to break them at all.

They coasted to a halt on a tree-clad hillside in Rivington from which they would get a good view of the western sky, but with enough shrubbery for them to become easily concealed.

They had missed the actual sunset, though the sky had not yet recovered from the experience, being still livid with colour. He climbed out of the car and opened her door for her. He took her hand and walked her over to a stone seat, where he removed his jacket and spread it for them to sit on. The western horizon was a mass of fading gold. Even as they watched, it grew crimson, splashing colour on the underside of a small fleet of clouds.

'Look at that sunset!' Judith gasped.

'Yes,' he said. 'Look at that sunset,'

As she turned to him, he took her chin in his hand. Their faces were very close. For one heady moment their eyes met, before his lips descended upon hers and his hand slipped downwards. The stone bench was cold and rough, so he drew her onto the grass, by a clump of bushes out of sight of the road and pulled up her skirt.

'Let's go home,' she gasped in desperation.

'Too late,' he said, unzipping himself.

Judith felt herself becoming completely lost. All the years of righteousness fell away like the shell of a hatching crocodile.

'We can't,' she moaned. 'I'll get pregnant.'

'Didn't you take anything?'

'No.'

What kind of woman did he think she was?

He swore and reached for the pocket of his discarded jacket. He started fiddling around with a rubber sheath.

'Can you – help me – get it on?'

It was then that they heard the giggling from the bushes and looked up to see the faces of two girls from the upper fourth.

He drove her back in silence. She sat with head down and back bent like the stem of a dying tulip. She could not speak. When the car drew up at her house she fled indoors without a word. The tattered shreds of her self-esteem to which she had clung for so long had been scattered to the four winds.

Chapter 9

Eileen phoned Lucy.

'Susie says Judith wasn't at school today. Has anybody said anything to you about it?'

'Not a word.'

'I went down the road to see for myself.'

'See what for yourself?'

'Nothing, as it happened. She was in bed. She wouldn't see me. You haven't heard anything?'

'What about, Eileen? What should I have heard?'

'I wish I knew.'

By Tuesday teatime Lucy had become tired of getting no answer by phone. She drove round to Judith's house and Wendy let her in. Judith was clattering around the kitchen looking wooden-faced and rather strange.

'Are you ill, Judith?'

'I've got a headache.'

'You've seen a doctor?'

'He came yesterday.'

'What did he say?'

Judith turned her head to the cupboard. The world would have to be faced. It was not going to go away.

'He gave me some tablets.'

He had also given her a note of absence for the rest of the term. Mercifully, the summer holidays were not far away.

'Well make sure you keep taking them,' Lucy said kindly, 'and we'll see you at band tomorrow.'

Judith closed her eyes.

Lucy left, feeling a bit brutal to be exerting pressure on behalf of the band when clearly

Judith had other worries. But she knew Joan and Deirdre were likely to be absent for most of the summer, because of the school holidays. Judith's presence was vital.

But brutal or not, on Wednesday there was no Judith. Neither was Wendy there and Lucy discovered for the first time just how inadequate the second cornet part was with only Rebecca. She had imagined that the older girl was carrying Wendy, but obviously it was the other way round.

It was a severe blow.

She struggled through a couple of hymns, once Annette arrived, which was late. The melody line was thin. She put up 'Tightrope Walker', in the hope that Florrie would carry them through. But the accompaniment fell apart. There were too many rests for the cornets during Florence's solo sections. Annette and Rebecca seemed constitutionally unable to come in in the right place. After going through a small section six times and failing to eliminate its faults, she gave them an early break and sank into a chair, feeling thoroughly defeated. Eileen sat beside her, unable to think of anything to say that was not irritating.

'I think I'll have to call off the rest of the practice,' sighed Lucy, resting her face on her hand. 'Then we can all go out and enjoy the lovely evening.'

The sun was slanting through the doorway with unwonted cheerfulness, golden and dancing with motes of dust. Even as they stared at it a figure stood there, black against the sunset, with feet slightly apart and right shoulder lower than the left, from the weight of something in the right hand, as if ready for a shoot-out at the Lazy T saloon.

Lucy thought she was seeing things. She shaded her eyes.

'Can I help you?'

The figure stepped forward out of the back-lighting, revealing a woman in her late twenties with a mop of dark hair, clad in jeans and a loose T-shirt bearing a picture of Stratford-upon-Avon. The object in her hand could now be seen to be nothing more threatening than a cornet case.

'My name's Ruth Anderton. Have you got room for another cornet?'

'What did you say?'

'Must I repeat it all?'

'No no no. No. Please. I'm pleased to see you. Come and sit down.'

Simmer down, Lucy told herself. Act as though this happens every week. 'Can you play a top part?'

'Try me.'

She opened the case and produced a run-of-the-mill Westminster cornet from which all the lacquer round the valves was worn off. That could mean that she played it a good deal; or it could mean that it was Grandad's and she had just found it in the attic.

'This is Annette,' Lucy introduced her. 'She's leading at the moment.'

'That's a trumpet!'

'Sorry about that,' said Annette insincerely, 'want me to leave?'

'Don't you dare!' hissed Lucy.

Then she called the murmuring room to order and everybody to her seat.

'Let's have a crack at the "Medley of Scottish Airs".'

Ruth asked Annette for her B, then her A, then her E flat. She adjusted her tuning slides to her satisfaction. Then she rippled up and down the chromatic scale prestissimo for two octaves. She saw that Lucy was waiting for her.

'It works,' she quipped.

Lucy raised her baton, caught the communal eye, and made the downbeat. Not a single entry was missed this time. The 'Keel Roll' was up to speed. 'Comin' Thru' the Rye' was played better by Annette than she had ever played it before. She had something to prove now.

Then as they approached the first pause, it suddenly occurred to Lucy what was coming and what could happen and on an impulse she stopped the band. Her intuition was right. A single note continued. It was only one long note, but it was immaculately shaped. There was a pause for breath and the Westminster sprang into life. Bursts of notes like clusters of fireworks rose higher and higher up to top C and beyond – even higher than was actually written, according to Lucy's score. The performer added a few curlicues and a flourish of her own, before she came cascading downwards to the point where the band was supposed to join in again. Instead they burst into spontaneous applause.

Ruth looked up in surprise.

'Wasn't I supposed to do that?'

'You can do mine as well if you like,' Mary told her wryly. She did not fancy having to follow that display.

Lucy looked at Eileen and Eileen smiled at her. They were both thinking the same – something on the lines of the darkest hour being just before the dawn.

Not that the band was not still under strength, of course, but with the newcomer they had the most crucial factor. The one which had always been missing, in spite of the trombones. The king pin. The keystone. The principal cornet player. From that time onwards they would be able to go through all the repertoire they had and nothing would need to be abandoned.

She dismissed them a little over time. Les and William sat and enjoyed the closing

'Eventide'. The purr of Harold Mackenzie's Jaguar had been heard through the open door. Now she must have a word with this strange woman just to make sure she could join them on a permanent basis.

However, she was waylaid by Florrie, who had a list of the order of service and of what was to be played and when and by whom. It was not straightforward, since the organist was to be there as well, for items like Mendelssohn's *Wedding March,* an arrangement of which they did not possess and in all likelihood would not have been able to play if they had.

By the time Lucy was free Ruth had gone, along with most of the others.

'Did she say she was coming next week?' she asked Eileen, who was one of the few remaining.

'She didn't say owt to anybody,' Eileen told her. 'She was out of that door like there'd been a four-minute warning.'

'Who is she? Where has she come from?'

'No idea.'

'Damn!'

It took Lucy the whole of Thursday to stop reproaching herself for not nailing the newcomer well and truly down. But at her age she had had time to learn that nothing in life is unconditional and that if the Good Lord sends the answer to a prayer it does not necessarily mean that there will be no more troubles to contend with.

For instance, the wedding was approaching with the inevitability of an oncoming tide. You think it will be ages yet, then suddenly the water is around your feet. She must retrieve her two established cornets and the baritone before then if possible. She wanted everybody to benefit from the experience of playing in public. With the wedding, they could make their debut using some relatively easy pieces of music. It is a good idea to take the nursery slopes before going on to the slalom.

Lucy arrived at the courthouse good and early on the morning of Sheena's trial. It was an intimidating building. She was glad she was there as a spectator and not as some miscreant about to feel the full weight of the British judicial system.

After an hour and a half of specious arguments and red herrings and bureaucratic sub-clauses as numerous minor offenders sought to evade, through their lawyers, the consequences of their patent guilt, Sheena's appearance was over surprisingly quickly. She walked out of the court room a free person. She did, however, have a suspended sentence hanging over her. The magistrate told her she was a lucky girl and he hoped she would take advantage of his leniency to build up a law-abiding life for herself, away from bad company.

It was fixed for her to stay with Lucy and Harry until such time as she could find employment and lodgings and become rehabilitated into society.

Steve and Adam were further remanded to be sent for trial. There was a long list of serious charges to be brought against them. Too long for a mere magistrate's court to deal with. They included possession of illegal narcotics and grievous bodily harm. Worse, the police were reopening the case of a certain body in a certain canal. It was likely to be some time before Steve took his place among law-abiding members of the general public again.

But at least Sheena had him to thank for her own freedom. Because both lads had insisted that she knew nothing about anything. So the police, who wanted to charge her jointly with some of the other offences, had to be content with unruly behaviour, resisting arrest and assaulting a police officer.

Lucy took her to the house in Babylon Lane to see if they could find anything that was hers. Steve's landlord had repossessed his property. The rent had not been paid for some time, so he was within his rights. When he saw the state of the place he had had the locks changed and workmen sent in to repair and redecorate.

The front door had been removed and a new one was to be seen propped against the wall waiting to be hung. So when they arrived, Sheena and Lucy had no problem gaining entry. A sound of sawing came from upstairs as a cheerful tenor informed the world that he had lost his heart in San Francisco. A pleasing smell of fresh-cut pine wafted towards them.

All belongings that had not already gone to the dustman or been burned were lying in a dusty heap in the hallway. The pile did not amount to much, but they rescued the transistor radio and some of Sheena's clothes. Most important of all, the baritone horn was there among the debris, sitting upright like a faithful dog waiting for its mistress's return.

'I reckon it knows where it belongs, that bari,' Lucy remarked as Sheena drew the black case from the rubble and gave it a quick dust over with an old pyjama top.

Sheena said nothing. It was not a good time to confess that the instrument really belonged to Adlington Secondary Modern.

The story of what happened between Mrs Cashmore and Mr Greenhalgh had soon spread through the school and it was not long before the whole of Babylon Lane was enjoying the details, along with the kind of extra juicy bits that people love to add. Eileen lost no time in passing the sorry tale on to Lucy.

So the day following the trial, Lucy dropped Sheena off at the Adlington Employment Office and took the opportunity to call in on Judith again. Wendy was at school. It would be all right to discuss delicate matters if Judith could be prevailed upon to do so.

There was no reply when she rapped smartly on the varnished beech front door. A pane of stained glass was inset with leaded lilies arching gracefully towards one another. Trying to squint through the distortions of this to detect signs of movement was an unsatisfactory business. She knocked a second and third time. There was still no reply.

She went round the terraced block along the cinder track which ran along the back yards, counting carefully until she came to Judith's back gate. The latch raised unobjecting to her hand and she walked through the back yard past a clothes line on which hung wetly a tablecloth, a couple of dresses and some underwear.

She passed the gritty front of the coal space and rapped on the back door. It had a net curtain over its window. She could not make out anything through it. She turned the knob and walked in.

'Judith!' she called, to make it quite clear that she was not sneaking in for nefarious purposes.

There was no reply, but there were sounds of movement from upstairs. Lucy went into the hall and Judith appeared on the stairs in a dressing gown.

'I was having a lie-in,' she said defensively. She looked a mess in worn-out slippers, hair that needed washing and no make-up.

'I came to see if you were all right,' Lucy called. 'I knocked, but there was no answer. So I walked in.'

Judith came wearily down the stairs. She knew Lucy well enough to know that she would not simply go away if asked to do so.

'Want a cup of tea?'

'Yes please.'

Lucy followed Judith into the kitchen. Wendy's breakfast dishes were still on the table, cereal bowl unwashed. Maybe the items on the clothes line had been there since yesterday. Lucy racked her brains for something to say that would help.

'How's the head?'

'It's all right. Do you take milk and sugar?'

'Yes please.'

Judith moved the dirty dishes to the sink, swept the oilcloth of crumbs with her hand and set the teapot on the table. She brought two cups and saucers from the cupboard, not even looking for her best china. It was impossible for her to feel more ashamed than she already did.

'We need you in the band, Judith. You and Wendy.'

Judith sat down and poured. All she said was, 'Do you want a biscuit?'

Lucy waved the fancy floral biscuit-barrel away.

'We had a really good cornet player turn up. She's called Ruth Anderton. You heard of her?'

Judith shook her head. She took a bite of custard cream and it tasted like sawdust. She would never finish it. She sipped some tea to help wash down the crumbs.

'Only she's very good. Plays like a professional. She keeps Annette in order, too. But as you know two cornets simply aren't enough. And we need Wendy. Wendy holds down that second cornet better than Rebecca does. And Rebecca must be all of four years older. She's a gradely little player, is your Wendy. We'd hate to lose her.'

Judith was silent. Wendy had been upset at missing band. She knew the child was suffering. It was all her fault. How could she ever face people again?

'I hope you'll feel able to come and join us, Judith. If only for Wendy's sake. You can play the rep part if you'd rather. Then you could sit behind the front cornets. But even if you sit at the front nobody is going to point a finger at you...

Lucy seemed to be getting nowhere. Judith's face was wooden. Her hands crumbled biscuit into her saucer.

Then the telephone rang.

Judith froze.

'Don't answer it!' she ordered.

'Is it him?'

'I can't speak to him.'

'Perhaps he's worried about you.'

'I don't want to speak to him.'

Judith's voice rose and wobbled and she started to shake.

Lucy went and picked up the receiver. A woman's voice asked for Judith.

'It's Mavis,' Lucy told Judith, keeping her hand over the mouthpiece. 'Will you speak to her?'

Judith shook her head.

'Phone back in about half an hour,' Lucy advised the voice. 'I'm with her now. She's all right for now.'

She returned, sat down by Judith and put a hand on her arm.

'She's going to phone you again at lunch time. There are a lot of people who care about you, Judith. You don't have to be alone. We're your friends. You know that, don't you. We're all human beings. We all have the same weaknesses. Anything that happens gets talked about for five minutes, then forgotten. Your five minutes are nearly

135

up. Don't shut yourself off from your friends.'

Judith put her head on her arms and wept. Lucy sat by and let her cry on. She did not know what more to say and maybe silence was better.

The following Wednesday Lucy made sure to call for Judith and Wendy in her car and ferried them to the practice in person, even though the Cashmore residence was within easy walking distance of the Spinners Arms and out of Lucy's way. The others had been forewarned to use kid gloves and friendly smiles. The Hetherington girls were too young to conceal their smirks altogether, but by and large everybody behaved towards Judith as though she had merely been off sick.

Only Ruth Anderton had not been informed of the situation, since Lucy did not know how to contact her. But in any case she had not put in an appearance by the time everybody else was settled and waiting to begin. It was a sad disappointment.

'Does anybody know anything about last week's new cornet?' she asked, without much hope of an answer.

'She plays up at t'Granary with that new group,' Rachel told her.

'I knew that!' Susie informed the room at large.

'Well why didn't you tell me?' Eileen wanted to know.

'You never asked me,' responded Susie, in chorus with half the room.

It was a relief to Lucy to know that at least somebody knew where to find her. She had not been a passing stranger riding into town, doing her good deed and riding off back into the sunset from whence she came.

For Annette's sake she started with 'The Old Castle'. She wanted to see how she would cope with Judith on the repiano part behind her. But Annette knew it quite well by now and though she was half a bar out on her second entry, she adjusted quite quickly.

As they finished, the door opened and in walked Ruth Anderton.

'Am I late?'

'We start at seven thirty.'

'Sorry. I assumed you started at eight o'clock. I don't know why.'

She seated herself on Annette's right and swiftly went through her warm-up procedure and Lucy felt sufficiently confident to ask them to put up 'Regimental Selection'.

Top cornets tend to work together by a system of sharing the solo bits, when they are not playing in unison to strengthen the melody line. They have to decide between themselves who is playing what. It is up to the leader to allocate.

After giving a strong lead in the first two repeats, Ruth shook the drops out of her instrument with a flick of the water key, while the euphonium took the Trio, then she sat back as the Da Capo approached and cried, 'Hit it, glamour girl.'

Annette hit it and hit it hard, if slightly off-centre, like someone who would like to have hit something else.

Afterwards she turned to Ruth.

'You'd better watch that mouth, stranger, or I might start calling *you* names.'

'All right. Sorry. Mum's the word.'

'Actually,' Annette retorted coldly, 'Mum isn't the word I had in mind.'

Instead of taking offence, Ruth gave a short, surprised laugh.

'I'm glad to see you two are hitting it off,' remarked Lucy, quite unconscious of any irony.

There were still a few places in the piece which needed taking apart and working on, but Lucy did not want to push their endurance too far. So she called a short break. Alice and Mary brought out their knitting, Winifred and Gladys their respective women's magazines and the young ones gravitated to a corner to chat. Annette sat as far away from Ruth as possible and busied herself honing her fingernails to a fine edge with an emery board. Eileen took it upon herself to engage Judith in friendly conversation, by asking her about suitable practice books for Susie.

Lucy seized the nearest piece of paper, which was an old shopping list from the bottom of her handbag. She smoothed out the creases and sat in Annette's vacated chair, a pencil poised in her other hand.

'Can you give me your address and phone number?' she begged. 'Just in case I need to contact you between practices. Yours is the only one I haven't got,' she added.

'Sure.'

Ruth took the pencil and scribbled down an address on the outskirts of Chorley.

Lucy took the piece of paper and memorised the address as a precaution, but still folded it carefully and placed it in a side-pocket of her handbag, very much as Mary had done with Eddie Pickerskill's promissory note. She felt a good deal more secure with that information in her possession, especially now that Judith and Wendy and Sheena were back.

She would be able to face the summer absentee season with more confidence.

Chapter 10

At last the Great Day dawned. Florence and Wilfred were to be joined in Holy Matrimony. The weather rose to the occasion. A heat haze hung over the meadows and there was not a breath of wind to stir the standing corn. August was poised to move in.

The band assembled in the church early, glad of the cool of the stone vaulted interior. Only the younger ones regretted having to come in out of the sunshine, as they left their instrument cases in the nearby church hall. In brightly coloured cotton dresses, they crunched up the gravel path, clutching cornets, horns and trombones. Bringing up the rear was a ginger-haired twelve-year-old dressed in pink, complete with large satin bow on the top of her head, embracing a huge bass. The procession caught the eye of a photographer. A picture appeared in Monday's paper over the caption: 'Brazen Ladies Entertain Wedding Guests'.

Once inside the church, they packed themselves into an awkward little space around the lectern, leaving room for the happy couple to pass to the altar – just. Cornets clinked. Music stands pinged as they struggled into place and sat fanning themselves with sheet music. Sight lines to the conductor were far from perfect.

'Everybody get where you can see me,' Lucy told them. 'If you can't see me, move to where you can.'

'Like the organ loft, for instance,' grumbled Susie. She was handicapped by having the fattest instrument to peer around. However, when she moved beside the carved oak post at the corner of the choir stalls she found a line between the heads of Sheena and Winifred, along which she could just glimpse the baton.

Lucy felt it advisable to give them a lecture about the evils of levity in a church. There was to be absolutely no giggling, or even whispering. This was a solemn occasion.

She had reckoned without Wilfred.

Clad in his best suit, he was perspiring freely in the front pew. They started to play their small repertoire of hymns and sacred pieces as soon as Lucy saw the first of the guests file in. When the pews filled up, the temperature rose. Wilfred pulled a large handkerchief from his trouser pocket, not wanting to disturb the neat triangle at his breast, and a handful of change went clattering over the stone tiles. He and his best man stooped to pick the coins up. Wilfred disappeared under the pulpit after some silver, then returned to his seat.

By now the band was well into Handel's *Largo*. Waving her baton limply by the steps, Lucy glanced across and saw that he had a black mark down one side of his forehead. She hung onto her straight face and dared not look again.

Eventually, there was a signal from the door. She slowed the band and stopped them at the next full cadence to allow the organ to spring to life with 'Here Comes the Bride'.

Florence had done things properly. Resplendent in glossy white, she had accentuated her already more than adequate height with a headdress that added a good three inches. Wilfred's two diminutive daughters followed her as bridesmaids. She towered regally above her father as they slow-footed it along the ecclesial carpet. Only the swish of tulle and muffled sobs from Charity could be heard above the organ. The scent of stephanotis marked her passing.

Sensing her at his side, Wilfred turned and gave her a big smile.

Mirth hit Florrie like a jab in the nibs. She strangled a cry. Even she dared not give vent to a peal of laughter at her own wedding. But she knew she would never make the responses. She had to act fast.

She whipped out the lace hanky, borrowed from Gladys and tucked into her bra. She spat on it. Then she took Wilfred's startled chin in her hand and rubbed at his forehead until the dirty mark had gone.

'Thanks,' he breathed in a puzzled voice.

Unfortunately, the band had had ringside seats for the performance. Even as the vicar announced the singing of *Crimond* they were dabbing their eyes and spluttering into their instruments. Lucy grimaced at them to pull themselves together as she raised her baton. She brought it down and all that happened was a rather disgusting parp from the E flat bass. Tucked away behind her wooden post, Susie had seen nothing of the incident and therefore was the only one in a fit state to form an embouchure.

From the body of the church came the faint murmur of discreet communal amusement.

The organist was reading the *Racing Times*, having been told to do only 'Here Comes the Bride' and the *Wedding March*. Hearing the silence, he took it that he had got it wrong and thought they must be waiting for him. In a panic, he quickly filled in the two last lines of *Crimond*, which he knew by heart, as an introduction to lead the congregation in. Then he saw in his mirror that Lucy's arms were raised. So he stopped, in order to leave them to it.

The band broke into *Crimond* a semitone lower and the confused congregation came in in dribs and drabs or not at all, sounding so pathetic that Florrie's shoulders began to shake, ominously. Wilfred, tense and nervous as he was, also felt an awful urge to laugh. He pulled out his handkerchief so that he could bury his face in it, pretending to blow his nose.

And the coins rolled out again.

Fearing a repetition of the previous incident, the best man grabbed his arm to hold him back and the sight of him being restrained caused someone to hiss, much too audibly, 'Wilfred's trying to make a run for it.'

By now the spirit of laughter was like a hungry lion, seeking whom it may devour; and most of the cornets and the flugel fell victim there and then, drastically cutting the melody line.

Lucy thought the last verse would never come.

At least Wilfred did not drop the ring. The responses went without any trouble, though the determined inflection in Florrie's voice when she said 'I do!' nearly set some of the band off again, in their weakened state. Then, after the vows, Wilfred trod backwards, forgetting that he was on a step, and was only saved from falling into the horns by the best man.

'Don't go yet, Wilf. Tha'll be missin' t'best bit,' came an anonymous voice and this time the whole congregation let go and roared with unseemly laughter.

After that things went smoothly, including 'The Lost Chord', which set Charity off sobbing all over again. The happy couple reappeared to the joyful strains of Mendelssohn. The organist was so determined to get it right that he was still playing it when everybody was outside and throwing their confetti.

Alice and Gladys went to be photographed along with the rest of the family and had to take their trombones with them so that they could hold them up in an arch over Florrie and Wilfred's heads. Mary and Les joined them with William, whose smart clothes were still in pristine condition. He flounced around shamelessly showing off his waistcoat and bow tie. Mary hoped the trousers would remain unscathed until they could find a toilet at the reception.

This was held at the Spinners Arms, of course. There was a help-yourself spread and flowers all over the place and waitresses in frilly pinnies and suave young men going around with bottles wrapped in serviettes to keep in the cold.

Tom quickly got a couple of glasses of champagne down to join the ale. Susie had rather rashly told him about how she had been the only one to come in on time for *Crimond*. Now he was telling all and sundry how sorry he was to have missed his daughter's solo number – 'The Queen Mary Leaves Liverpool Docks'.

'It was only funny the first time, Dad,' Susie told him scornfully as she walked past with a plate of trifle in one hand and a tumbler of champagne in the other.

The place was packed with animated talkers, red in the face as the temperature rose. Women with handbags slung over one arm were balancing disposable plates and trying to eat vol-au-vents without getting flakes of pastry down their cleavages. The necks of bottles would appear by people's elbows and fill up their glasses without them noticing.

Rachel's mortification at having no boyfriend to bring vanished because nobody noticed who was with whom among so many. All the younger ones, including Sheena, gravitated to the same corner – near the food and drink. They teased one another and flirted with the opposite sex. Susie's brothers, Stuart and Philip Riley, with whom Rachel and Rebecca were not supposed to associate, pelted them with nuts and cheese straws. They had jelly tipped on their heads in retaliation. It was great fun!

Annette was there, eating daintily and 'showing her legs' as Gladys put it, in a skirt two inches shorter than anybody else's. Harold stood beside her trying to look as if he was enjoying himself. His Saturday afternoons were usually better spent than standing around with a lot of people he did not know and who were unlikely to be of the slightest use to him in the world of business. But at least the rugby season was over, so he was not missing seeing Wigan play.

Their three sons hung around like dogs unaccustomed to the leash, behaving like civilised human beings, on pain of fatherly wrath. Timothy, who was ten, was told to go and talk to Wendy, who was looking a bit lost. Judith had gone straight home. Playing with the band had probably saved her sanity, but the social stress of a reception was an ordeal she was not yet ready to face. She had asked Eileen to see Wendy the short walk home.

Timothy found the girl very hard work. He could not seem to make any conversation stick and had to content himself with going off and finding her some ice cream. He did not know that she was afraid of boys. At school she only played with other girls. She knew that boys could be rough and dangerous. She could not tell which were the ones to be avoided and which were not. So she avoided them all. Now something bad had happened to her mum and all to do with that Mr Greenhalgh.

However, the youngest of the three Mackenzies eventually melted the ice. Nobody could be afraid of six-year-old Christopher, who had his mother's smile. He grabbed Wendy's hand and pulled her over to where the sausages on sticks were just out of his reach and asked her how she'd learned to play the trumpet and told her that his mum sometimes let him have a blow on hers and when he was older he was going to be the best player in the school and when he left school he was going to play in a band – for money – and he would be very famous and could she dish him out a large helping of that sherry trifle?

Mary regarded Annette from across the room – her beauty, her rich husband and her three healthy, clean and well-behaved sons. Why did some people have so much?

Soon Florrie and Wilfred reappeared in their going-away outfits. They were going to catch the train to Blackpool. Wilfred sported an ancient moleskin waistcoat that had belonged to his father. Florrie, on the other hand, looked really smart in a well-cut floral summer dress. The station was, as you might expect, at the bottom of Railway Road, so the newly-weds walked the distance, accompanied by all the guests, almost bringing the Saturday afternoon traffic to a halt. Attracted by the noise, people came out of their houses to wave. Their children swung on their gates, those that had them.

'Have you got your music?' Harry asked Lucy. 'A marching band is just what's needed. The final touch, like.'

'Keep your voice down,' begged Lucy. Just walking straight was challenge enough for her at the moment. But at least she was walking, unlike Susie, who had pleaded heavy bass and had to be left behind, collapsed over three chairs.

Adlington Station, a two-line affair which trains of any stature would whizz straight through, was seldom graced with such a colourful crowd. The train steamed up, snorting and hissing. There were enough helping hands to make sure that Wilfred climbed onto it with his bride and that it was, actually, the right train for Blackpool.

'Look after Aunty Charrers for me,' Florrie called to Alice, who stood behind the wheelchair, as they climbed aboard.

'Will do,' shouted Alice, blowing a kiss.

'Make sure Wilfred doesn't get off at Preston.'

That was Gladys, of course.

'I've got him chained to my wrist.'

'Already!'

The train shuddered and hissed and noisily the wheels began to turn. As it started to move another shower of confetti missed them and landed on everybody else.

Mr and Mrs Robinson waved from the window as the train gathered momentum, then the platform gave way to a grassy bank which was lurid with Rose Bay Willow herb. They sank back onto the seats. It was good to be alone.

Until the door slid back and a crowd of noisy youths pushed in. They put their feet up on the seats and brought bottles of beer from their pockets, removed the tops and started swigging. They belched without inhibition and their language was not a pleasure to hear. Furthermore, they opened the window without asking if anybody minded and trod all over Florrie's feet while leaning out of it.

After all, it was Saturday afternoon.

'Let's all have a sing-song!' cried Wilfred. He broke out into 'Now is the Hour' and Florrie piped up in harmony, throwing him off the tune.

Before the end of the first verse, they were alone again.

'So how did it go?' Harry wanted to know. 'The church service?'

'Very well. The congregation was very appreciative.'

'Everybody had a good cry, I hope,' he persisted.

'Believe me,' Lucy told him, 'there wasn't a dry eye in the place.'

Chapter 11

How Lucy and her ladies missed Florence the following Wednesday! As with Wendy, her true worth was only appreciated when she was not there. Alice and Gladys still made a good team, and with Joan and Deirdre putting in an unscheduled appearance, there was plenty of strength up top. But the underpinning was gone. To make matters more difficult, they could no longer afford to spend the practice doing easy music. The wedding was past and gone. Sterner tests lay ahead. They had to gird up their loins for deeper waters, as Lucy told them, conjuring up visions in one or two heads of happy days at the seaside.

They must start digging the foundations, she continued, for the mountain they had to climb, as well as they could with the holidays now in full swing. The syllabus for the next Spring Festival would be out in September. When it did she would know which compulsory piece had been set for the small bands class. Meanwhile, she would have to decide which of their limited repertoire she should select for the 'own choice' item. Anything in four parts would not be considered adequate, so all the hymns were out of contention.

She knew from her experience with choirs that to perform something simple well would always go down better with an adjudicator than making a mess of something more difficult. That eliminated 'Regimental Selection'. 'Tightrope Walker' was their most audience-friendly number, but it featured one player. They would be judged as a band and in a competition all sections should be used. That left 'The Old Castle' and 'Scottish Airs'.

She decided upon 'Scottish Airs' and worked on all the bridge passages, leaving out the cadenzas because she knew they were in good hands. They had to be. She was relying on them to add a touch of class to set off what she hoped would be the well-drilled teamwork of the rest.

After thoroughly exasperating all her bandswomen with a series of stops and starts and making individuals go over bits they had been hoping to leave out altogether, she gave them a break.

They relaxed, sighing with relief, and dispersed to their odd corners.

Ruth, who felt that her lip had hardly done enough blowing to extinguish the candles on a one-year-old's birthday cake, produced a book of advanced exercises, set it up on the stand in front of her and attacked one of its

152

most strenuous pages. Halfway down, she became aware of a pair of eyes riveted upon her from a distance of about two or three chairs away. She looked up to see Wendy, open-mouthed. She gave her a quick smile and moved on to the next exercise. Wendy sidled up to her elbow and stared at the page.

'How do you do that?'

'Do what?'

'That.' Wendy pointed to the correct note-packed line on the page. 'I could *never* do that,' she added.

'Yes you could,' Ruth reassured her. 'All it takes is years of practice.'

'Yes, but how do you *do* it?'

Ruth explained about triple tonguing. She made Wendy imitate the sound without the instrument; then she made her try it with the mouthpiece alone. After that she let her attempt to make the same sound through the cornet on the note of G at a much reduced speed. The attempt was a bit spluttery, but obviously on the right track.

'That's it, kiddo! You can do it, see,' Ruth encouraged her, which had the effect of making Wendy fall over herself in the attempt to achieve perfection immediately. 'Slow down, slow down. Never go too fast. Speed will come in its own time when you're ready. You've got the right idea. Just keep practising at home and you'll soon notice the difference.'

'She doesn't have time for that just now,' cut in Judith from behind them. 'She's got exams next week.'

Judith had applied for a post which had providentially become vacant at St Hilda's School for Girls just outside Bolton. Their music teacher had had a heart attack and died after working too hard on a stiff reed for one of her oboe pupils. If Judith was successful it would be the answer to a prayer. But she was tense and nervous about it. It was an independent school. Wendy would be having to sit the entrance exam.

'I can practise *and* study, Mum. I always have.'

'No you can't. Your exams are too important,' said Judith rather brusquely. She was much more snappy than she used to be. Moreover Ruth was so full of her own importance and Judith was more than ready to find someone she could dislike more than she disliked herself.

Wendy was a little taken aback by the unfamiliar harshness in her mother's tone. Ruth was positively offended.

'Relax,' she said. 'It's only triple tonguing I'm teaching her. It's a perfectly harmless activity.'

She slung her Westminster into its case, clicked it shut and walked out, leaving Judith scarlet with mortification.

'What happened?' Lucy wanted to know, rushing up in dismay.

'I don't know,' quavered Judith, beginning to shake again. Anything seemed to make her shake these days. She picked up her handbag and grovelled desperately for her bottle of tranquillisers. 'I'm sure I didn't say anything very bad.'

Lucy ran outside in time to see a pale green Hillman Minx turn out of the car park and onto the main road.

'I'll go straight round and talk to her after the practice,' she told Eileen, who was standing supportively by the door. 'Lucky I got her address, wasn't it? I'll ask Annette to run Sheena back for me.'

When Lucy mustered her battalions once more after their break, she realised that 'Regimental Selection' was *hors de combat*. Thank heavens for 'The Old Castle', she thought; until they tried it and found its foundations were very shaky without the bass trombone. Something would have to be done about Susie's tuba. The girl blew with a will and was quite fearless, but the poor tuning was undermining the sound of the whole band.

'All right. Get out the hymn books.'

She would ask Eileen if Tom could take another look at it.

As soon as they had all packed up and the

last handbag retrieved from the top of the piano, Lucy climbed into her Mini, turned its nose in the direction of Chorley and spurred it into action.

There were more streets in the new estate than she had realised. She had to cruise round a couple of times, getting slightly hot and bothered, before she found the right place. She parked the car on a curve of kerb and walked up the path, rehearsing a few blandishments about Judith and the need to make allowances for her and to please not imagine that this was an habitual state of affairs – no, she could not seriously say that out loud. She knocked on the door.

At first she thought that she had come to the wrong house after all. The woman who answered was not Ruth. She looked more thirty-ish than twenty-ish. She was very thin and had green-brown slanting eyes. She managed to convey sexiness without conventional good looks.

'I'm looking for Ruth Anderton. Have I come to the right place?'

'Yes.' She called over her shoulder. 'It's a lady for you, Ruth.'

'Well ask her in, then,' reproached Ruth, appearing behind her. 'Oh, it's Lucy,' she added. 'Lucy, this is Sarah.'

'Pleased to meet you,' said Lucy.

'Sarah?' she thought.

They shook hands politely and ushered

Lucy into an immaculate lounge, decorated in tasteful pastels with all the right matching carpets and curtains. It looked a place in which no child had ever set foot. It was quite sticky finger free.

'Want a drink?'

'No thanks...' began Lucy, then realised that a drink was just what she needed. She added hastily, '...or maybe a gin and orange, if you've got one.'

Sarah went to the drinks cabinet in the corner. Ruth sat her down in an armchair.

'I've really come to find out what happened,' Lucy began. 'You left so suddenly. I hope Judith didn't upset you. She's had a bad time lately and we're all trying to make allowances for her.'

'I'm glad to hear it.'

Lucy waited, but nothing else was said. No guideline was thrown for her to pick up. She blundered on, feeling increasingly uncomfortable. But it had to be done. She had to sort it out.

'I don't know what she said to you, but please don't take any notice. I mean, you haven't left us, have you? You will be back, won't you? I mean, your playing is really valued.'

Why did she feel so hot? It must be her Time of Life. She wanted to take out a tissue and mop her forehead, but that would only draw attention to the fact that she was perspiring like a candidate for an aural exam in July. There was something about the stillness between them, as if they were communicating with each other without words. She felt at a disadvantage but did not know why.

'I enjoy coming to your band, Lucy,' Ruth broke the silence. 'It's useful to me to be there. Keeps me in practice. Keeps my playing up to scratch.'

'That's good.' Lucy took a sip of her drink.

'Only one thing you must all understand is that I'm not interested in little girls. Any more suggestions of that nature and you won't see my exhaust pipe for fumes.'

Lucy looked from Ruth to Sarah and from Sarah to Ruth. They returned her gaze with identical eyes. She felt like Doctor Foster on his way to Gloucester – except that she had not stepped gingerly into a puddle right up to her middle, but sunk in way over her head. The hairs on the back of her neck bristled. What did a person say in these circumstances? She realised to her dismay that the glass she was clutching was now empty.

'I'm sure none of us would ever suggest such a thing!' she protested.

The silence that followed was fraught with embarrassment – hers and theirs. She looked at her watch. She must get out before she made matters worse. She rose to her feet.

'Thank you for your time,' she said, lamely. 'I must be getting along and – we'll see you next Wednesday, then.'

She hastened out into the cool night air and the comforting familiarity of her little car.

'Damn!' she swore to herself as she zoomed away.

Ruth stood in the doorway, sadly watching her hurried exit.

'Damn!' she said.

Sarah joined her and put a hand on her shoulder.

'She didn't know, did she?'

'Looks like it.'

Ruth closed the door.

'They probably didn't mean what you thought,' ventured Sarah, picking up the empty glass.

'I know,' agreed Ruth. 'But they will next time.'

Lucy put the car in the garage and picked her way to the front door, wetting her calf on a dew-covered overgrown laurel bush. They really must get that outside light fixed, now that the evenings were starting to draw in again.

A midweek fixture was being shown on the telly as she walked in and put her stack of music on the piano next to the framed certificate which informed her pupils – and their parents – that she was a Licentiate of the Royal Academy of Music.

'Did Sheena get back all might? Did she tell you where I was?'

'Shhhhhhh!'

She could hardly be heard above the rising tide of commentator and crowd as the winger centred a pass, the inside left lobbed a cross and the centre forward headed for goal.

He missed.

Not wanting to hear Harry's reflections on the matter, she went to take her coat off and make herself some coffee. She was no stranger to the odd gin and orange, but was not accustomed to demolishing them quite so quickly.

There was no milk. Sheena had scoffed the lot. And the biscuits. Well, she could make a black coffee and it would do her more good. But she was getting tired of Sheena's little ways. She never tidied her room, she finished off cereals and, less forgivably, bottles in the drinks cupboard, and never told anybody. So nothing was ever there when you wanted it. It really was time that she got a job and moved out before somebody blew her top. Worse, Harry might blow his. Especially if she kept playing music late at night on the trannie she had rescued from the house in Babylon Lane.

'Why am I doing all this?' Lucy began to ask herself, especially after as stressful an evening as this one had been. She and Harry were well-off. Their daughter was at university. They were not yet old enough to be in their dotage. This could be the best time of their lives. Yet here she was lumbered with all these problems. And all to do with this band, which had not been her idea in the first place. What was she doing it for? Why did she not pack it in?

Then she thought of Mary and her courage and her refusal ever to complain. It was for her and for William. But more than that – because there must be other ways to get a van for handicapped children – lobbying the local health authority, for instance. It was for Alice, whose life was not very interesting. It was for Winifred, who was lonely; for Judith, who needed support; for Wendy who needed encouragement. It was for Florence, who loved it, and even for the Hetherington girls, who would most likely forsake it for the World of Boys soon enough, but who in the meantime could be kept out of mischief. Well, on Wednesday evenings, anyway.

Later on, when Harry joined her in bed she was able at last to gain his attention. She poured out her account of the evening's doings, staying his wandering hand until he had listened.

'It's not the end of the world,' he reassured

her, reconciled to the fact that he would get nowhere until she had unburdened herself of her thoughts. In any case, the sound of Sheena's radio was killing off his amorous feelings.

'Maybe not. But don't tell me it can't make a lot of trouble.'

'Well I dunno. I've met one or two blokes like that in my time and it seems to me that they're only trouble when they're looking for a spot of what they fancy with their own sex. Sounds like this one has already found it.'

'That's certainly the impression I got.'

'Well I reckon you've got nothing to worry about,' he reassured her, if only to put an end to the conversation. 'When that sort of person is fixed up with someone they can be no bother at all. That's my experience, anyway.'

'I'd say she was well and truly fixed up. Well and truly. So let's hope you're right.'

Chapter 12

The next day Wendy got up early and was puffing away at her cornet at the crack of dawn. Judith lost no time in taking her out shopping. But all the way there the child was saying to herself t-t-k-t-t-k-t-t-k, quite softly, but never quite inaudibly. It was the same coming back up the road at midday, and she could not be distracted for long, even by questions like 'What do you want for your birthday?' Judith longed to tell her to shut up. She had been going to teach her daughter triple tonguing herself when the time was right. Obviously the right time had arrived and somebody else had got there first. But she knew it would be wrong to put a damper on her enthusiasm.

Once inside the house, Wendy went straight to the cupboard and took out a book of technical exercises which Captain Higginbottom had lent her and found a page of triplets. Then she took out her cornet and, standing up good and straight in front of the open book, she worked and worked at her triple tonguing.

Judith went into the kitchen and ran a glass of water to wash down a couple of tranquillisers with. Then she put the radio on, so that she did not have to listen to the struggles in the next room. They formed a faint counterpoint, which she could just ignore, to the afternoon play. She found a jigsaw puzzle in the bottom of a cupboard and forced herself to fit it all together while she listened to a good old-fashioned detective story.

Wednesday duly came around again and Lucy's car drew up outside their front window. There was no need to hoot. Wendy's face was plain to see peering around the net curtain.

'I can do triple tonguing,' she shouted excitedly as she scrambled into the back of the Mini over the front passenger seat. 'Want to hear me?'

'Since you ask, no!' replied Sheena, who was occupying the other half of the rear, filing her nails.

'When we get into the band room, Wendy,' Lucy told her.

They soon arrived and Lucy made it her business to encourage Sheena to help set out the chairs while people arrived. The girl had a strong tendency not to be of any use whatsoever. All right, so she had had a bad time. She had had a rotten upbringing. She was disadvantaged. But Lucy was a firm believer that doing a disagreeable job well was a good way to make yourself feel better. It gave you a lift just to get it out of the way.

The Ainscough van could be heard groaning into the parking place outside. But it produced only Alice and Gladys.

'Isn't Florrie back yet?'

'Oh she's back all right,' Gladys assumed them.

'She doesn't travel with us any more,' pointed out Alice, a mite sadly, 'but she'll

164

surely be here soon. Takes more than marriage to keep her away from her trombone.'

Lucy opened her case and pulled out a sheaf of music. They still did not have as many pieces as she would have liked, though things were improving in that direction. She could hear somebody running through advanced exercises, so she composed her features into the impassive expression with which she was determined to greet Ruth.

However, when she turned round, there was only Wendy intent on the page before her, rattling through a whole series of semiquaver triplets with an expression of utter concentration and her feet hooked round the chair legs because her legs were as yet too short for them to be placed comfortably on the floor. Teenage sisters Rachel and Rebecca came crashing through the door, but Wendy did not notice.

Lucy glanced at Judith, who was watching her daughter with a mixture of pride and despair. Gradually the whole room became quiet. Wendy grew conscious of the attention which by now was directed upon her from every quarter and started to fluff a few notes. She coloured up and stopped.

'I can do it better at home,' she informed Lucy.

'Can't we all!' commented Rachel sourly.

'That was very good, Wendy. I can see you've been practising,' Lucy commended her, keeping a casual tone. But she knew, and she could see that Judith knew, that the child was gifted and should not be left to flounder on alone any longer.

The door burst open and Florence breezed in, greeting everyone loudly and looking quite pink and girly. To the inevitable 'How's married life?' she replied, 'Haven't you found that out yet?' whatever the inquirer's marital status.

Ruth Anderton walked in quietly and sat in her place, not wanting and not receiving any attention. She took out her cornet and warmed up under cover of the general hubbub.

Wendy called to her from three seats away. 'I can do triple tonguing,' she piped. 'Listen.'

Wendy set off again on her exercise, but in her eagerness to please she made quite a mess of it. She sighed in annoyance. She had been waiting all day to impress Ruth.

Ruth, however, had been through the same process in her time. She recognised cause and effect and was still impressed. But was it wise to give the child the attention she craved? She shot an anxious glance at Judith, was reassured to see that she was not looking and ventured to give Wendy an encouraging smile.

'That was a good start, kid. You spoiled it because you were going too fast. Take my tip

166

and slow down a bit. Remember – let speed come in its own good time.'

She turned away, opened her music stand and set it on the floor.

'I can do it better than that. I did just now. Let me show you again.'

'Better not,' Ruth advised, sighing inwardly. 'Keep your playing for the band. Otherwise you'll end up tired before you start. Now if you'll excuse me, I've left something in the car.'

She rose and went outside as a means of escape.

The room was filling up. Or was it the entry of Eileen and Susie with the E flat bass that made it seem fuller? Lucy pursed her lips. That was the next item on the agenda: What to do about the bass. She crossed to where Eileen was unpacking her tenor horn.

'Did Tom have another look at Susie's bass?'

'He had a look at it. Gave it a bit of Brasso and put a proper spring on the water key, instead of the rubber band it had before.'

'Is that all?'

Lucy's knowledge of E flat basses could be written on the tip of her baton, but she could not believe that those measures would improve its intonation.

She was right. When they started to play it sounded all the more frightful because she was listening for it. So was Florrie, who succeeded in drowning it out at the expense of her own tone. But there were times when her instrument was resting. It takes more stamina to play than a bass and is therefore given more rests. So then she had to endure helplessly the desperately mistuned notes much too close to her ears.

As they tramped to the last bar of 'Regimental Selection', Florrie could contain herself no longer. She laid her trombone carefully on a row of chairs and asked to have a blow on the offending instrument.

It sounded little better.

'Is that the right mouthpiece?'

'It's the only one it's got,' Eileen told her.

'It's smaller than mine. I reckon that's a euphonium mouthpiece. Look, Mary...' she added, removing it from the mouth pipe, where it was wedged in tightly with folded paper, and holding it out to her sister. 'Is that not a euphonium mouthpiece?'

Mary removed her own mouthpiece and they compared the two.

'Aye, they're t'same size. Look at that.'

Lucy came close to inspect them.

'Is that going to make a lot of difference, then?'

'It'll certainly make it sharp.'

'Where can we get a proper sized one, then?' Eileen wanted to know.

'School should have one, surely,' suggested Gladys. 'It's their instrument. It must

168

have had a bass mouthpiece in t'first place.'

'Yes, but things disappear at schools,' said Rachel darkly. Sheena surveyed her through narrowed eyes, but the remark did not appear to have been directed at anyone in particular.

'In any case, it would mean waiting till September and I, for one, don't fancy that prospect,' said Lucy.

'Nor me,' was Florence's heartfelt agreement.

She went to her case and brought out her spare. It was the one she had used for the G bass and much inferior to the more modern one which had come with her good new one. It was a bit too wide and deep to get the higher notes on the B flat part of her instrument, but she had been fond of it once and had kept it 'just in case'. It was certainly larger than the one Susie had been using.

Florrie put the school one aside and inserted her old silver bass trombone one into the E flat bass. It was a better fit. It did not have most of the shank disappear into the mouth pipe like the previous one. It stuck out further, in other words. She blew a ponderous scale, unaccustomed as she was to using valves. It was certainly an improvement. She wiped the mouthpiece on her sleeve and replaced it in the mouth pipe of the bass with a small piece of the paper wadding.

'Try that one for now, Susie. You can give it me back when you get a proper one.'

Susie took it good-naturedly. She did not mind criticism. Praise she would have found it harder to cope with. She played an extra loud C to make them all laugh again, but nobody did, because surprisingly it was not bad enough to be funny.

'Right,' chipped in Lucy, before Susie broke into the 'Dance of the Elephants' or something similar. 'We'll do "Regimental Selection" again. Let's see if it sounds any better.'

It did.

In fact, it turned out to be rather a good practice. The sound was growing fuller as the players grew in confidence. Having Ruth at the top and Florence at the bottom made up for many little weaknesses elsewhere. Some of their music was by now quite familiar to them. Just as important – it was also more familiar to Lucy, who had had time to identify the trouble areas and work on them.

When she stopped them for their customary break, she addressed them before they had time to divide into chattering groups.

'I thought we might have a concert this Christmas. Would you all like that?'

There was a general murmur of approval.

'You mean a real concert – with an audience?' Susie wanted to know.

'I regard an audience as an essential part of any concert,' Lucy informed her gravely, to some laughter. 'At that time of year we could play mostly carols. We could make it a whole evening of carols,' she continued. 'Get the audience to join in, if they wanted to. Then we wouldn't be jumping in at the deep end with all the difficult stuff.'

'Have to recruit some scuba divers,' quipped someone.

'Tuba divers,' added somebody else.

'Well I reckon it's a good idea,' Eileen rushed to her support, before the jokes got out of hand. 'Get us used to playing in public.'

'I was hoping it might also make a bit of money,' Lucy told them. 'Then whenever the band needs anything – like a proper mouthpiece for the bass, for example – we'll have the resources to get it.'

Susie reinforced the point with a new, improved, bottom G.

'Thank you, Susie.'

'We could hold a raffle.' That was Mary. 'Raffles always make money.'

'Good idea.'

'And Wilfred can be Master of Ceremonies,' suggested Florrie.

The room was filled with nays.

'No offence,' said Lucy, 'but I'd prefer it if he had pressing business in Aberdeen that night.'

171

'I've got some holidays coming up,' Annette felt it necessary to inform her. 'I'll have to be away for three weeks.'

'I dare say you're not the only one, Annette. But thank you for telling me. We'll have to miss a Wednesday anyway for the Adlington Wakes Week. That's in a fortnight's time. Anybody else with holidays come and tell me at the end of the practice and I'll write them all down. Then I won't forget. All right. Take your break.'

They broke up into groups. Alice and Mary sat in a corner with their knitting. Winifred joined them. Gladys went to the Ladies for a smoke. The younger ones sat on the apron of the stage and swapped gossip. Ruth asked Annette if she could have a look at her trumpet.

'Don't tell me I'm out of tune, please,' pleaded Annette languidly as she handed it over.

'Not at all. It's a lovely instrument. I'm green with envy. Where did you buy it? Not at Chorley market, that's for sure.'

'Harold brought it back from New York a couple of Christmases ago.'

Ruth looked impressed. Her eyebrows disappeared into her hair.

'Does he often go there?'

'He goes all over the place. Wherever his work takes him.'

Ruth turned the instrument to read the

trade name on the bell. She flexed the valves and did everything except actually blow it.

Lucy watched them. Eileen followed her gaze.

'Are you going to break them up?'

'Break them up?'

'Well we don't want them getting too cosy, do we?'

'What do you know about it?' snapped Lucy. She had told no one except Harry about Ruth's predilections.

'It's all over the Lane, Lucy. I mean can you see Tom keeping a thing like that to himself? It's the best bit of material he's had since the Lady Mayoress fell down Bolton Town Hall steps.'

'Nothing's going to happen in the band room, Eileen,' Lucy told her, crossly. She would have a thing on two to say to Harry when she got home.

As if to underline her words, Annette rose.

'Have a blow on it if you want to,' she offered Ruth. 'Be my guest. I've got to go and pay a call.'

And she disappeared into the Ladies.

Chapter 13

August went its fickle way and some of the population managed to get a bit of sunshine between bouts of summer rain. Lucy had been looking forward to having her daughter Rosemary home. She had hoped that she could take Sheena under her wing and, optimistically, that she could lead her into better paths than the ones she had been treading. But Rosemary had phoned in early July to say that she was going to stay with a friend in Kent at the end of term and they would be making a trip to Italy together, to help with their studies. She would not be home until after the August bank holiday.

So Lucy and Harry took Sheena to New Brighton for the day, going through Liverpool and taking the ferry across the Mersey estuary. The girl did her best to enjoy their company and their conversation, conscious as she was of how much she owed them. But her eye was constantly drawn to groups of young people. She kept thinking she saw Steve – the back of someone's head – the way he walked – the jacket he wore. He was no good. She knew he was no good. But she still wanted him.

She felt trapped in the company of an older couple, but there was nowhere better to go. New Brighton was not noted for La Dolce Vita. If she had been on her own she would have picked up a bloke soon enough. She was no good. She knew she was no good. Like Steve. They were made for one another. The short time they had been together she had felt like a fish in water. It was the only time in her life she had felt like that. She missed him like crazy.

When Rosemary did return, Lucy tried to get Sheena to mix with the younger set. But Sheena had nothing to contribute to a group which was better educated, better brought up and far more socially acceptable than herself. The gulf was too great. They were kind to her but she felt utterly inferior. The spirit of rebellion began to stalk her, like a creature that knew a good bit of prey when it saw it.

Eileen and Tom took their children to Morecambe, where Stuart and Philip went off to do adventurous things, grudgingly towing little sister around the amusement arcades, where they almost succeeded in losing her. Their parents sat around in deck-chairs watching the tide retreat over the quicksands before they went to listen to the band.

Mary and Les took Alice and Gladys to Belle Vue Zoo with William for the August bank holiday. The place was a bit too crowded for Mary's liking. They had to queue to get in, queue for ice cream, queue for the toilets and crane their necks to see the orang-utans. William enjoyed the reptile house. An obliging python was sloughing its skin. Gladys gave a shudder and went off to see the parrots, but William stared for ages at the brightly coloured snake slowly emerging from a crumpled old skin. Les stayed with him while Mary and Alice went to join Gladys. They stopped for tea, then they all went to see a show at the ice rink and came back late, singing through the dark journey home, as the street lights flicked past, one by one.

Judith had managed to land the post at St Hilda's. She spent the latter part of the summer moving house to where she would be but a short bus ride away from her work, thankful to leave both Adlington and its Secondary Modern School behind her. Her new home – another middle-terrace two-up two-down – was on the route of the bus which passed her school on its way to Bolton. When it went in the opposite direction, bound for Chorley, it stopped directly by the Spinners Arms. So she would have even less distance to walk to band practice than when she had lived a hundred yards away down Railway Road.

Florrie and Wilfred took Old Bill and Aunt Charity to Blackpool. Charity was determined to have her ride on the Big Dipper. Bill said he had learned a bit of sense in his old age and would be quite content to throw all his money away on the rifle ranges while the others took their pleasure frightening the living daylights out of themselves.

Of course the funfair was very crowded. It had been the wrong day to come. There were queues at most of the rides, including the Big Dipper. If trade had been slack the man in charge might have been prepared to be lenient, but with so many to cater for he flatly refused to allow Charity on. He knew that if anything amiss happened he might find himself in court. Florrie dragged Wilfred away as she saw him opening his mouth. There were too many people waiting. It was not the right time to make a fuss.

Charity was deeply disappointed.

'Never mind,' said Florrie. 'We'll go on everything else.' They hoisted Charity into a dodgem car and Florrie squeezed in beside her. Wilfred took another one and they chased one another all over the floor. Until he got stuck in a corner, trapping several other cars with him. They enjoyed the boat-like swing that gained height with each to and fro until it was almost ready to do a full circle. They survived the 'whip', that spun even as it circuited on a slope. Encouraged by Charity's happy face, they took her on the Octopus – a device with revolving modules at the end of long arms, which swung around and up and down, until the passengers were completely disorientated. Charity took it quite well, but Mr and Mrs Robinson emerged green and shaky-kneed. Once they had hauled Charity back into her waiting wheelchair, they felt quite glad to forget all about the Big Dipper.

They picked up their dad at the shooting stall. In spite of his arthritis he had won a four-foot-high panda. With difficulty they crammed it and themselves and Charity's collapsible wheelchair into Wilfred's shooting brake and they all had a good laugh chatting about the day on the way home.

The second Wednesday in September found all the band members present and correct – well, fairly correct – in the band room, ready and eager to get to grips with a programme of music fit for the general public to hear. Lucy had asked Alice if they had enough money in the Handicapped Van collecting tin to purchase a full set of books of carol arrangements.

'The band'll pay you back with a bit of interest after the concert – that's assuming we'll make any money, of course.'

Alice was quite happy about it. So was Mary. After all, a person had to speculate in order to accumulate.

At her own expense, Lucy had also acquired the set piece for the festival. It was called 'Prelude to a Storm'. She had leafed through the full score with growing concern, wishing she had got hold of it earlier – or that they were not doing it at all. There was far too much percussion. However, the die was cast. They would simply have to find the resources somewhere. There was no way out but through.

'I hope you've all been practising,' she greeted them, regarding with satisfaction face after face.

'What are we starting with?' Ruth wanted to know. 'Not a certain selection of regimental marches, by any chance?'

'Believe me,' Lucy told her, 'when you've seen what we've got for the second half you'll be begging me to give you "Regimental Selection".' She smiled at all the falling faces. 'So enjoy all these carols while you have the chance. Hand the books round, will you, Rebecca? And we'll start on page one.'

They were almost too easy. To avoid boredom, Lucy concentrated on tone and tuning. Then she chose verses in which the cornets could remain silent so that another instrument could take up the melody. She gave some of 'Once in Royal David's City' to Mary's euphonium. The trombones just had to have 'We Three Kings of Orient Are'. She asked Rachel to take the second verse of 'Silent Night'. The tone of the flugel was perfect for it. Should she find a solo for the tenor horn? She would check it out with Eileen privately. Panning the players to see if she had covered the possibilities, she caught the eye of Wendy, positively pleading to be chosen.

'What would you like to play, Wendy?' she asked.

'"O Little Town of Bethlehem",' came the prompt reply.

'With all those flats?'

'I don't mind flats.'

'All right, we'll give it a try.'

Of course, Wendy played it beautifully. Mary did equally well with hers. The trombones added a delightful touch of humour to the proceedings. But when Rachel's turn came things did not go so well. Although it was possibly the easiest piece to play, her approach was nervous and therefore tentative. With a brass instrument you cannot be tentative. She made a complete mess of the high bit near the end.

'Work on it at home, Rachel,' said Lucy kindly, before she called a break.

Rachel retired to the Young Person's

Corner with mortification and a general rage against the unfairness of life burning in her heart.

Lucy called together Florence and Ruth and Judith to form a team of consultants about various aspects of the concert. She felt it was important to stay in touch with the views of those who knew more about brass than she did.

'I was wondering,' she put it to them, 'about the best way to get variety into the programme. That's why I've given solos to some of you. Has anybody else any ideas? Or suggestions for pieces? If we can get hold of them, that is.'

'If I were you,' ventured Ruth, 'I would invite at least one guest who has nothing to do with brass – a pianist, for example.'

'Or a children's choir,' suggested Florrie. 'Just think of all the parents that would bring along.'

'Can you supply one?'

'Not me, no.'

They looked at Judith, who cringed inside. She shook her head. At her old school she had never been able to keep the choir in order, still less bring them to a standard to be heard outside the school portals.

'I haven't been at St Hilda's long enough,' she excused herself. 'I'm not sure how the suggestion would be received.'

Lucy thought of her Women's Institute

choir. Would it be wise to mix the two? If anything went wrong she would be doubly humiliated.

'I'll look for a soloist,' she told them.

Wendy sat reading a comic. There was nobody else of her age to talk to. Nobody, even, to impress while Lucy's conference was taking place. A shadow fell on her page.

'Are you having lessons from Ruth Anderton?'

She looked up to find Rachel regarding her in a manner she could not give a name to, but which made her feel most uncomfortable.

'No.'

'Why not?'

Wendy did not reply. She was being tricked into something and she did not know what it was.

'I should ask her,' Rachel continued with a spiteful smile. 'Go on. Ask her. I bet she'd love to give you lessons.'

'I don't think my mum would let me.'

'Why ever not?'

'I – I – I – don't know.'

Wendy felt suddenly ashamed, without knowing why.

'Of course, a cornet isn't something most girls would take seriously – most *normal* girls, that is.'

'Oh?' Wendy loved her cornet.

'Most of us just play for fun.'

The child looked back at Rachel from behind her wire-rimmed specs. Her mouth was open and her eyes bewildered. Rachel felt she had made her point. She returned to her sister and whispered something in her ear that made her giggle.

For the rest of the evening Wendy could hardly put two notes together.

Lucy handed round the parts for 'Prelude to a Storm'. As far as possible, she was going to have a straight run-through without stopping, unless they ground to an unscheduled halt. She had a red pencil in her right hand and was going to conduct with her left. She intended to write down comments in the margin as they proceeded, which she could check on when she was back at home. She would then have the leisure to try to work out what the particular problem was and what was the best way to deal with it, so that she could come back next week with tactics at the ready.

Of course the task proved impossible. The difficulties were too complex to be writing notes and trying to read the score at the same time. In the end she settled for a stop-start run-through and they were just about able to reach the end. Two things stood out. The first was that the instruments they did not possess were going to be needed. The second was that Wendy was not coping with her part at all well. What was the problem? Really somebody ought to take talent like that in hand. The child was crying out for a good teacher.

They disbanded and went their separate ways homeward. Judith stayed to help with the chairs as usual and as a result missed one bus and had a twenty-minute wait for the next. Lucy offered them a lift home.

'It's out of your way.'

'Oh hop in,' Lucy ordered them, opening the passenger door. 'It's starting to rain.'

So Wendy climbed into the back seat of the Mini beside Sheena and Judith took the front passenger seat, slamming the door on a corner of her coat. Lucy asked her about St Hilda's and what the standard of music was like there and what part of the syllabus she was required to teach, while Wendy sat huddled and quiet in the back, thinking her own thoughts, until they were interrupted by Lucy.

'What do you want to be when you grow up, Wendy?'

'I – I don't know,' she stammered, wishing she could be left alone.

'She's only just ten,' put in Judith.

'Has she thought of taking up music as a career?'

'Do you think that's a good idea?'

'She has the talent.'

'Can you turn right here?'

'If you don't mind,' Wendy decided to speak up, 'I don't think I want to.'

'You're much too young yet to know what you want.'

They pulled up outside Judith's house. Wendy wanted to get out, but was trapped in the back.

'Can we get out, Mummy?'

Judith opened the door and unfolded herself into the road.

'Think about it,' said Lucy, as Wendy clambered over the forwardly angled front seat. 'You've got plenty of time.'

'No. No, I don't want to.'

Wendy sounded as if she wanted to cry. The two women watched as she scuttled up the short path.

'I'm sorry if I spoke out of turn,' said Lucy. 'Is anything wrong?'

'I haven't the slightest idea,' sighed Judith. 'I just don't understand anything any more.'

When Sheena failed her sixth job interview, Lucy decided to take matters into her own hands, for the sake of Harry's sanity and her own.

'That lass really knows how to put the *"loco"* into *"loco parentis"*,' Harry complained when he discovered there was nothing to wash down his chips with. 'What's she want with brown ale? It's no drink for a slip of a girl.'

'It was there,' said Lucy simply, 'and she's got nothing to do.'

'Well find her summat for crying out loud. There must be summat she can do. Waitress. Shop girl. Anything.'

It was not easy. Everybody knew about Len Grimshaw and his drinking and his feckless daughter and her bad associates.

Lucy confided in her hairdresser on her weekly Friday visit and it turned out they needed a girl to make the tea and sweep away hair clippings. Their usual lass was about to go away for some serious training. Lucy seized the chance and fixed up for Sheena to go in the next morning. She would take her there herself to be certain there would be no slip-ups.

Chapter 14

On Monday Susie came home from school, slammed the door and threw her satchel into a corner, knocking over the plant stand so that it scattered peat across the floor. Ignoring it, she stamped loudly upstairs.

Eileen stood in the hall with her hands on her hips.

'Now just you get down here and clear up this mess, young madam, do you hear me?'

Susie stumped down again with a face like thunder. 'What's the matter?' Eileen wanted to know. Susie was not given to tantrums.

'It's not fair!' complained the child, dragging a hand-brush and dustpan out from under the stairs, with total lack of grace.

'What's happened? Have you got a detention?'

'It's Mr Jenkins. He's taken my bass and given it to one of the boys. It's not fair. Boys always get what they want. I hate boys!'

The door opened and Stuart came in, so Susie threw the brush at him. Stuart, hot from the cricket field, deftly caught it with his free hand, made as if to aim it at the stumps, but began to juggle with it instead.

Eileen frowned at Susie.

'Now say you're sorry, Susie.'

'Sorry,' murmured the miscreant in a low voice, genuinely ashamed.

'That's all right,' Stuart told her airily. 'I used to hate girls when I was your age. They always get let off all the horrible work.'

He handed her the brush and went whistling to his room, while Susie swept up the peat.

It was not just the loss of the instrument that concerned Lucy.

'What's happened to Florrie's mouthpiece?' she wanted to know, when Eileen turned up to the next practice.

'Gone with the wind instrument, to quote Stuart.'

'But can't Susie get it back?'

Lucy glanced anxiously at the door. Alice and Gladys were out of earshot. Florrie had not yet arrived.

'She says she'll ask. But I think I may have to go to the school myself in the end. The trouble is,' she continued, 'Mr Jenkins is an old gentleman, apparently. Retired. Used to teach at a boys' public school. Doesn't like to see a little lady making a fool of herself, he said. Would you believe it? Susie's done nothing but play the fool all her life. Good job he wasn't at the Guides' Jamboree! They'd have had to carry him off on a stretcher. On second thoughts, perhaps it's a pity he wasn't there.'

'But he's only temporary, then?'

'Until they get a proper replacement for Joe Greenhalgh. He gave Susie a viola. Said she would be welcome everywhere if she played a viola. I doubt it. She hates it. After having it around the house so do I. Tom says if she sat on the roof she'd have every cat in Adlington joining in.'

'He's got no right to go messing things about like that!' fumed Lucy, referring to Mr Jenkins. 'It's not his place to make policy decisions if he's only holding the fort.'

'Try telling him that.'

'It would be simpler to get her a bass of

her own.'

'Or even get a bass for the band,' hazarded Eileen, who did not dare ask Tom to pay for a bass when he was always so quick to make mock of their efforts.

'Any idea what they cost?'

'A lot, I think.'

'I was hoping to use any money we made to buy a bit more music.'

'Yes, but we can't enter the Brass Festival without a bass, can we.'

Lucy sighed. She would have to give the matter some thought. Meanwhile, there was a practice to be taken. It looked like they had a quorum of musicians, so Lucy told them to put up the 'The Old Castle' and after a short spell of tuning, she gave the downbeat. Florence pumped out the bass line loud enough to make four tubas redundant. But she had too many rests. After a few minutes of the rather hilarious contrast between thunderous bass and no bass at all, Lucy stopped them and stood with one hand on hip and fingers to mouth wondering whether to give a B flat bass part to the euphonium. But Mary's part could not be spared. Perhaps the second trombone?

'If you want to give me the E flat bass part, I can play it,' offered Florence, seeing her dilemma.

'It needs transposing,' Lucy warned her.

'Not into bass clef, it doesn't. I just add

three flats.'

That was good news indeed. She handed Florence Susie's old part and they launched themselves from the ramparts again. This time they took some semblance of flight.

However, there were untoward noises coming from the direction of the second cornets. Lucy kept glancing that way and noticed a certain amount of inattention. Once she caught Wendy miming something silly to try and make Rebecca laugh. She never used to be so badly behaved. Was Rebecca having a bad influence? Should she put one of them onto third cornet? Which one? She had better consult Judith before burning any boats.

When she mentioned it at break time, Judith told her that Wendy had not practised all week, which had never happened before. That was strange, but there was no time to pursue the matter further. More urgent issues were waiting to be addressed, and now was the time, while all the women were present. Lucy coughed and clapped her hands a couple of times to draw their attention, before revealing what had happened to Susie and her bass.

'I have to say,' she continued, 'that unless we have at least one bass – we ought to have two, really – but without any we can't enter the festival. And if we did we would stand no chance. Has anybody any ideas about where we could find one?'

A rare silence descended upon the ladies. Not even a futile suggestion was made. They looked at one another and remained dumb.

'It isn't fair to ask Eileen to get one,' Lucy added. 'A bass costs more than any other instrument. It will benefit the whole band. Not just the person who plays it. So I think that the whole band should share the cost, if they can. What do you think of that?'

'What sort of cost are we talking about?' Gladys asked in a hedging kind of voice.

'I can't say until I've made enquiries. And even then it would hit some people harder than others. But how about if any of you felt you make a donation – those that can – towards the cost – and after the concert, the band will reimburse you – assuming we make anything out of it, which I'm sure we will.'

'You mean loan, rather than donate?'

It occurred to Lucy that she could be getting into deep water.

'I'll keep a record,' she told them, with more assurance than she felt. 'I'll make a note of everything.'

'We ought to have a treasurer,' suggested Mary, feeling that Lucy should not be carrying so much extra responsibility.

'Want to volunteer?'

'Well I...'

'Show of hands, please, unless there's anybody else wants the job.'

Nobody did. The hands went up. While Mary was still working out the best way to say no, she was elected.

There was little they could do on the 'Prelude' that evening. It was valuable time lost. A decision would have to be made soon as to whether they could enter or not for the coming March. It would have to be made before their carol concert, which was a pity, because playing in public would have proved the acid test as to whether they could acquit themselves with pride or disgrace themselves with shame. In any other circumstances Lucy wouldn't have committed her under-strength band, but they needed to beat Great Hulme Motors next March or not at all – unless Eddie Pickerskill could be persuaded to extend his deadline.

Now lacking a proper bass, she had to content herself with finding a section of the set piece where the horns and euphonium had some tricky interchanges with the trombones. She concentrated on the tenors and the baritone, giving them no chance to miss anything out, much to their chagrin. Then she went through 'Scottish Airs' just to make the cornets feel it had been worth-while coming and called it a night.

Rachel waited impatiently inside the porch for Rebecca, who had decided to go to the toilet before leaving. As if she could not last out until they were home! It was less than half a mile up the road, but Dad insisted that they walk together.

Lucy, meanwhile, was putting chairs back where they came from, helped by Eileen and Judith. Wendy in her usual helpful way carried some one at a time. Her journey took her close to the door. Lucy was by the piano, but she thought she heard the words 'Ruth Anderton' and when she glanced across, Rachel's look of malice and the distress on Wendy's face suddenly made a lot of things clear.

It was fortunate for Rachel that Rebecca turned up to join her sister just then, enabling her to make a quick exit, when she took one look at Lucy approaching with a face of granite. Lucy let her go. After all, she could not afford to lose her flugelhorn, which she might if she came out with all the invective that was forming in her head. The important thing was that she now knew what was wrong with Wendy and could start trying to repair the damage. She gathered her belongings together, called out to make sure nobody was still inside, and left, locking the door behind her.

She was surprised to find a Jaguar car still in the parking place. Its door opened and Harold Mackenzie got out. He strode over to Lucy.

'Got time for a word?'

Lucy's heart sank. No more problems, surely.

'Is it important?

'My wife tells me you're having to buy a bass. Replace an old one. Is that right?'

'Yes.'

'She suggested I offer you an interest-free loan. I can get you one if you want one. Then you can go ahead and buy one to keep practising with and pay for it in instalments – makes it easier. Don't have to be without your bass while you save the money. Of course you can go to one of the loan companies if you want to – I'm not trying to push business onto you. Just an offer, you understand?'

'How kind of you,' was all Lucy could find to say. 'Interest free? Can you really do that?'

'That's what I said and that's what I meant. No catch.' He smiled at her, his grey eyes inscrutable in the lamp light. 'Annette tells me all about your band, you know. All the difficulties you have to face.'

'Where would you go to buy a bass?' Lucy asked Harry the next day, when he had finished his tea. He was always in a better frame of mind when he had eaten.

'New or second-hand?'

'New if it's not too costly. Otherwise second-hand.'

'There's the trade magazines. You could advertise. Or there's *Exchange and Mart*. Or one of the big music shops.'

'Susie's had her bass taken away. Did you know?'

'Aye. I heard about it.'

'Did Tom say anything about her having to get another one?'

'If I had my way,' Harry said testily, shaking out his paper as a hint that he wanted to be left to read in peace, 'somebody would take all your instruments away. This damn silly business has gone far enough!'

'Silly!' Lucy was stung. 'It's not silly when it's your colliery band.'

'If you can't tell the difference, love, it's no use me trying to point it out to you.'

And it's no use me arguing, thought Lucy. Be more constructive to find Sheena some lodgings. That was what was really bothering him. She went to the kitchen, where Sheena was taking an unenthusiastic drying cloth to the dishes that were stacked and dripping on the draining board.

'How did you get on at work today?'

'All right,' mumbled Sheena, for whom the day had dragged by on leaden feet.

'Listen. If you want anything to drink, ask me. Don't take it from the cupboard. Harry gets upset if anything's not there when he wants it.'

Lucy did not want to get like some

landladies she knew; the ones who would plaster their apartments with notices:

PLEASE DO NOT SLAM THE DOOR, or PLEASE DO NOT LEAVE WET UNDERWEAR ON THE RADIATORS, or IF YOU WISH TO USE THE BATH PLEASE ASK DOWNSTAIRS FOR THE PLUG.

However, she was beginning to sympathise with them. Sheena was longing for Saturday. She would have some real money at last. She knew exactly what she was going to spend it on.

Susie was also longing for Saturday. On Friday Lucy, Mary and Eileen spent a couple of hours together with several directories and a telephone, making enquiries at every music shop they could find within a thirty-mile radius.

So when Saturday came, armed with the details of various available E flat basses, Tom and Eileen set off in their trusty Singer with a tank full of petrol, a supply of maps and Susie in the back seat with Mary, who had been given a cheque by Harold in her capacity as band treasurer. An account had been opened and her cheque book had arrived in the morning post. Two signatures were required. Eileen was there to supply the other one. Susie was going to be allowed to test out the possibles, but the adults would have the final say in the matter.

They began in the back streets of Ince-in-Makerfield, where news of an instrument for sale privately had been passed on to Tom via his band connections. It took them an hour to find the place, which upset their careful schedule straight away. The bass was quite badly dented and in such urgent need of a skilled welder that it nearly fell apart when Tom picked it up.

At a shop in Wigan, on the other hand, they were offered a gleaming object of tempting price. It was apparently brand new, but Tom had heard stories about that particular make.

'Last thing they told me at work was don't get a Chinese junk,' he explained to his daughter as they drove back north along a minor A road.

They had a bite to eat at Tessa's in Chorley, before driving to Blackburn, where the shopkeeper had a second-hand Boosey Imperial that looked much-played, like Ruth Anderton's cornet. Tom asked if Susie could be allowed to blow an F sharp, which was the same as A on the piano. He picked up a handy tuning-fork and hit it on one of the new pianos, causing the shopkeeper to wince. The note was nowhere near.

'That tuning fork gives an F,' the shopkeeper told him, snatching it out of his grasp.

He played a low A on the piano keyboard. Susie blew another F sharp, recognisably the same note! She blew down to low G. Then as high as she could. Then the B flat scale. It was not an offence to the ear.

The price was only just within the loan. They had hoped to use some of it for more musical pieces.

'What do you think?' Eileen asked Tom.

'We've still got Accrington, Rawtenstall, Rochdale and then back through Bury and Bolton. There's a good one on offer in Bolton, so they tell me.'

'All that way?'

'I like it,' was Susie's contribution.

'I tell you what,' offered the shopkeeper, sensing a sale, 'I'll knock two quid off, seeing as it's for the little lass.'

Eileen and Tom looked at one another.

'We'll think about it,' said Tom. 'We'll let you know.'

'Don't take too long about it,' he warned them. 'It'll soon go. There's plenty brass players around these parts.'

They left the shop and climbed back into the car. All of them wanted to go home. But nobody said so.

The Saturday traffic was becoming heavy. The football crowds were out in force. Kick-off time was approaching. How many stadiums would they have to try to crawl past on a circuit that included Accrington,

Bury and Bolton? What would it be like at five o'clock?

'I wanted that bass,' Susie complained, while they were still struggling to get out of the built-up area. 'I liked it.'

Tom looked at Eileen and Eileen looked at Mary.

'Let's see if he'll take a fiver off,' she suggested. 'A fiver less'd be reasonable. And I've still got Eddie Pickerskill's tenner if we're pushed.'

So they turned through a couple of back streets and got temporarily lost. By four o'clock all three of them were ready for home and its comforts. But they found their way back to the shop and the man agreed to take not five but another two pounds off and the band had its own E flat bass, with valves that worked smoothly and a comfortable, well-worn, proper E flat bass mouthpiece.

Chapter 15

On Wednesday Susie was able to create a stir by entering the band room triumphantly pulling the new bass behind her. It was in a bass-shaped case of its own. What is more, there were two small wheels on the lower corner, so that even a going-on-thirteen-year-old like Susie could transport it from A to B without having to pick it up. What a boon!

Eileen followed her at some distance. Her pleasure at the band's acquisition was tempered by a nagging worry over Florence's mouthpiece. Since Susie was no longer included in the school band and would never be ready for orchestra on her viola, she had no occasion to see Mr Jenkins. Nor did she make it easy for herself. She did not fancy knocking on the staff-room door, and when she passed him in the corridor, instead of going up to him and asking politely for the return of the substitute mouthpiece, she had dodged into the cloakroom out of his way and then re-emerged to pull ugly faces at his departing back. Too bad for her that her form master spotted her as she jumped up and down in the corridor with her fingers stretching the corners of her mouth.

Then she really did get a detention.

'I'm sorry about your mouthpiece,' Eileen grasped the nettle and cornered Florrie. 'But I will get it back, I promise.'

'I hope,' she thought. She knew how difficult it could be to trace objects when they disappeared into the school's all-consuming maw.

'I never used it,' Florrie reassured her. 'Don't worry too much.'

'All the same. If something happened to

the one you use...'

'I'll give it extra security by not lending it to you, Eileen,' Florence told her bluntly.

Mary was absent. William had a temperature and Les had been called upon by his firm to do some well-paid overtime. Her part was not important during the carols, where she was covered by trombone and baritone, but if they wanted to do 'Scottish Airs' or 'The Old Castle' it would be like driving a car on three wheels. Lucy decided to take a risk and offer the euphonium part in 'Scottish Airs' to Sheena for this evening. It was needed more than the baritone. Would Sheena make a mess of it, feel a fool and give up coming to band for good? You never knew with her.

'Just give it a go,' Lucy encouraged her. 'Just put the important bits in. I know you're sight-reading. It doesn't have to be perfect. Oh, and leave out the cadenza.'

'All right.'

In fact she made a good enough job, though she left out some of the higher notes and stumbled over the semiquaver runs. Nothing that practice could not cure. There was a tune called 'Comin' Thru' the Rye' which was written for the soprano. Lucy was hoping to have a soprano cornet player join them for the concert. In the meantime, since it was cued in B flat for the top cornets, Lucy wondered whether to give it to Ruth. But Ruth had plenty of big moments. Why not the trumpet? Why not Annette? She used to play it nicely before Ruth appeared on the scene. Moreover the Mackenzies deserved some special recognition after helping in her hour of need.

It worked well. It added some extra colour. Not only that, but Annette had quite a good ringing tone on the top notes which made the melody line sing out. Lucy almost wished the trumpet could be used for the festival without them being disqualified thereby.

After the Airs, it was time to put in some serious work on the festival piece. Which section of the 'Prelude to a Storm' could she work on this time? There was no question about it. Joan and Deirdre had turned up, bless them, making a special effort because they knew the concert was drawing near. She had decided to be brutal and put Rebecca on third cornet, retaining Wendy on second. She explained to the two part-timers that one of them was needed to help Judith on repiano and the other could sit on Annette's left and help the two top cornets. Unwisely, she left them to decide for themselves which went where and precious time was lost while they urged one another to the top bench. In the end she told them to take it in turns, starting with Deirdre.

A good deal of useful work was done, because the cornets had some difficult fanfares, and every one of the section, down to Rebecca on the humble third, was called upon to produce her share of the harmony. That was why it was a set piece. There could be no passengers. The timing of these fanfares required great concentration, since the note lengths were irregular and often syncopated. It was a case of rapping out the rhythm again and again with the baton on her stand until it was drummed well and truly into every head. She lost the end of her baton, but it was worth it.

Afterwards, she rewarded those on the larger instruments by going through 'Tight Rope Walker' and 'Eventide'.

As they stacked away the chairs at the end of the practice, Lucy asked Judith whether Wendy was having any piano lessons.

'Do you think she should?'

'Most certainly.' She raised her voice to include Wendy, who was passing a few feet away. 'Wouldn't you like to learn the piano, Wendy?'

'Oh yes,' Wendy agreed brightly. After all, perfectly normal girls often took the piano quite seriously.

'Would you like to take her on as a pupil?' Judith felt she was obliged to ask.

'I'd be pleased to.'

In spite of Florrie's protestations, Eileen felt that some kind of effort had to be made to get back the old bass trombone mouthpiece. She wrote a note to the headmaster of Adlington Comprehensive and gave it to Susie to hand in at the staff room. It brought an immediate response. Susie came home with the original mouthpiece, the school mouthpiece, the one nobody wanted, with which she had been forced to labour for so long. Not Florrie's.

The bass was no longer an issue for Lucy, who was not involved in the Great Mouthpiece Chase. But the problem of the percussion was the next to be addressed. A set of drums was not vital for the carol concert, but it would be for the festival. And the concert was a kind of dry run for the festival.

So on Tuesday, when Lucy faced her WI choir, she decided to take the bull by the horns and cast her hat into the ring.

'I'm looking for a lady with a set of drums,' she announced as they stood clearing their throats and preparing to tackle Brahms.

By the blankness of their faces she knew she had taken them by surprise.

'Nobody any ideas?'

'Do you mean timpani or a drum kit?' one bright spark wanted to know.

'A drum kit, of course, as in bass drum,

snare drum, top hat and cymbal,' she explained patiently.

There was some whispering in the second sopranos.

'What is it? Speak up! Don't keep it to yourself.'

'Our Jason's got a drum kit,' said a voice. 'Would he do?'

'Will he let you play them?'

There was general hilarity. Lily was small, plump and bespectacled and was only in the second sopranos because she could not reach the highest notes, nor pitch well enough to be among the altos.

However, there were no other offers, so the following Wednesday she was brought along to the Spinners Arms by her son, who was tall and as thin as a matchstick man. He stood over her all evening, beginning by playing himself, then handing her the drumsticks and standing ready to grab her arm, sighing with exasperation as she failed to get it right.

He was not, Lucy noted with a sinking heart, beat-perfect himself.

It was a laborious process and a bit of a hindrance to the practice, but surely it could only improve. She decided not to take them through the 'Prelude'. They were not ready for it. They went through 'Scottish Airs' and 'Tightrope Walker' and a couple of simple marches, which was all the drums were going to be needed for in the concert. Then Lucy sent mother and son home with appreciative words. What else could she do?

'Thank you for giving up your time, Jason. Practise as much as you can, Lily. And we'll see you next week.'

Then they concentrated on carols for the rest of the evening.

Eileen prevailed upon Tom to phone Susie's headmaster. Somehow fathers always cut more ice than mothers in these matters. He was on night shift this week, so was able to phone during school hours.

Once he had got through to the right person, he explained who he was and said there had been a mistake about the E flat bass mouthpiece. The wrong one had been returned.

'I'll speak to Mr Jenkins and phone you back.'

Much later the phone rang.

'Mr Jenkins says they have the right mouthpiece. The one he returned to Susie was the wrong one. That is to say the right one. It didn't fit the bass, so I understand, so it couldn't have been the school's. The one we kept fits the instrument, so it must be ours.'

'Nay it's not. The one the school gave Susie with the bass was wrong. It didn't fit. You gave the poor girl a euphonium mouthpiece and naturally she couldn't play in tune. She was kindly lent a better one. It came off a bass trombone. The one you've got now is a bass trombone mouthpiece.'

How could anybody make it clearer than that?

'Sorry, but I understand the one we gave you was more like a trombone mouthpiece.'

'That's because it's a euphonium mouthpiece. Same pitch as a trom.'

Tom was finding it hard to keep his patience, but he tried.

'I'll get Mr Jenkins to phone and explain it to you himself.'

The voice had the kind of placatory tone commonly used for fools and awkward customers.

But there was no call from Mr Jenkins. Tom sat down to tea with his family. He was in his work clothes, ready to venture out into the murky evening to start his day. Working nights was a miserable business.

'Somebody's going to have to go to that school and have it out with Sunny Jim,' he groaned. 'And it's going to have to be me.'

'Is that not Florrie Robinson's mouthpiece?' asked Philip, nodding towards the object on the mantelpiece.

'No,' his mother told him. 'That's the one the school gave Susie. It's not a bass mouthpiece so they don't want to know.'

'I reckon they know very well,' said Tom. 'Or that Jenkins comedian does. He just won't admit it.'

Philip said no more. But the following morning he pocketed the mouthpiece as he left for school. Alan Upton was in his class. Him as had the bass.

Lucy had done some research on the girl players in last year's festival. The soprano player lived in Wigan, which was a bit far to be coming to practices, but would pose no problem as far as a festival appearance went. After some correspondence with the parents, it was agreed that the girl would play with them if Lucy sent her the part to look at. She would then turn up during the Christmas holidays, if Lucy would ferry her back and forth.

The euphonium player was an older girl, a sixth-former. She lived just outside Warrington and was prepared to join them in their carol concert as well as another practice or two over Christmas. Again the price to be paid was transport.

The bass problem was yet to be solved, along with the extra horns.

When Philip came home from school, it was a different mouthpiece which he placed on the mantelpiece. Then went off whistling to do his homework. He was pleased with himself. He would surprise everybody at teatime, he thought.

Unfortunately it was only minutes later that Tom rushed in, smoothing his shower-damp hair with both hands, flung on a jacket, picked up the mouthpiece and rushed off to reach the school before the end of their Friday band practice.

It was easy to find the rehearsal room. All Tom had to do was follow his ear. Mr Jenkins was expecting him. When he saw Tom enter he dismissed his players, asking Alan Upton to leave his bass where it was for now. Then as the last child filed out of the room Tom tried to get the facts across again. It took a good deal of explaining and arguing, but the two mouthpieces were there, so, despairing of ever getting his point across, Tom simply took the one from the bass and put down the other on the conductor's stand. He dropped it into an inside pocket and walked out.

'You can sue me if you like!' he called, knowing that Mr Jenkins was quite aware of the rights and wrongs of the situation.

At tea-time he plonked his new acquisition cup-side down on the table.

'There you are, Susie. Don't say I never do anything for you.'

'I don't say that, Dad. It's Mum as says that.'

Eileen picked it up.

'I'll give it straight back to Florrie tonight. Thank goodness...' She examined it. 'Are you sure it's the right one?'

'It's got to be. It came off their bass. I took it off myself.'

'Did you get it from the mantelpiece?' Philip wanted to know.

'I got the other one from the mantelpiece. That's where it was put – on the mantelpiece.'

'Why?' asked Eileen sharply, seeing the look of dismay on her son's face.

'I took it to school this morning.' Philip explained. 'I swapped it while Alan Upton wasn't looking.' They were not pleased.

'Fancy doing a thing like that without saying owt.'

'I was only trying to help.'

'You didn't succeed,' Eileen told him.

'I had the devil's own job getting that blasted thing,' complained Tom. 'I'm not going back to that school.'

'Philip can do it,' put in Susie.

'Oh no. They'll kill me.'

'You swapped it once, you can damn well swap it again,' Tom told him.

They had football on Saturday morning. It could be the perfect time. The school would be open, but few people would be about. The bass would still be there, it seemed, in the hall. So Philip and Stuart set off down the road on a raw, sleety Saturday morning with their football boots slung over their shoulders

210

and the mouthpiece in Philip's pocket.

The first time he was tackled during the game, Philip rolled around on the grass clutching his stomach and allowed himself to be led, doubled up, back to the changing room. Once he had been left alone to recover, he changed quickly and made a beeline for the hall.

It was open. The chairs were still set out for band and some of the larger instruments were still there, including a couple of basses. Susie's was easy to spot, being the most decrepit. But when he went to exchange mouthpieces, an empty mouth pipe greeted him. Somebody had taken the precaution of removing the sought-after object.

'Screaming sardines!' snarled Philip.

On the long uphill road home he told Stuart about it.

'What are you going to do now?'

'Start saving pocket money, I suppose.'

Behind them a group of lads were plodding the same course, rather more noisily. They began to make mocking noises, which could only have been directed at the two brothers.

'We've got the mouthpiece!' someone sang out in the time-honoured sing-song cadences.

Philip glanced over his shoulder.

'Looks like the Friends of Alan Upton Society.'

'Do you reckon they've got it with them?'

'Could be.'

'Tell you what,' Stuart told him. 'Give me that there mouthpiece; the one you've got in your pocket. Then mark Alan Upton whatever happens, OK?'

'Right you are.'

Philip understood the footballing term. He handed it over. Stuart started tossing it up in the air and catching it, just a few inches at first and as soon as they sang out, 'We've got the mouthpiece', he replied with, 'Oh no you haven't!' to the same tune. He threw it a little higher, facing them and walking backwards.

For a while the two chants were flung backwards and forwards, as the group closed on Stuart and Philip.

'There's six of them,' Philip hissed.

'Shut up,' Stuart told him. He flung the mouthpiece so high that he had to run and catch it. Then he held it up in his hand so that they could all see it. 'Look!' he cried. 'This is yours. You can tell. It's shorter. Yours is longer. That means it's a trombone mouthpiece.'

Their strenuous denials were peppered with insults, but it had the effect he had intended, which was to cause Alan Upton to get the other mouthpiece out of his pocket and examine it. Stuart did not give them any time to think about it. He started to run up the road, taking his mouthpiece with him and chanting, 'Ha ha ha ha ha, I've got the mouthpiece.'

With all the predictability of Pavlov's dogs they charged after him, leaving Philip and Alan Upton staring after them uncertainly.

'You gonna give me that thing or am I going to have to take it?' Philip challenged him, standing in his path as he made to follow his friends.

'You can have it – here!' shouted Alan, and hurled it over the wall.

There was a splash. It had landed in the canal. Philip clambered up the wall and peered over. He could see the spreading rings where it had fallen. A barge was approaching.

'Want to follow it?' cried Alan, trying to push him over, but Philip jumped back down and hit him hard in the mouth. It hurt his knuckles but it hurt Alan more. Blood ran from his lip and tears sprang into his eyes. He turned and ran.

Philip walked up the road, nursing his hand. Stuart was limping down towards him, one eye red and swollen.

'He threw it in t'canal,' Philip told him.

'The little sod!'

When they reached home Eileen looked at them in some concern.

'Who were you playing? Attila the Hun?'

'And his army.'

Chapter 16

The carol concert was to be held in the back room of the Spinners Arms, where they were accustomed to rehearsing. There was a stage area at one end, which was really just a dais and did not even boast any curtains. But who needs curtains for a band? They could walk on in orderly fashion and receive the applause as they did so.

Their practise on Wednesday was the last but one before the event. Lucy asked them all to wear white blouses and black or navy skirts. Failing a uniform, it was the combination that was least likely to tax their wardrobes. The posters had been printed so she gave each of them a small sheaf to dispose of as prominently as possible. Harry was going to take the door money and Tom would usher people to their seats.

All there was left to worry about was making sure they had a full evening of enjoyable, well-rehearsed music. Or so Lucy thought.

Lily, the newly recruited percussion player, turned up at half time, as requested, and her son Jason set up the drums during their break. Then he stood back and left her to it, though you could see his hands were itching to get the sticks.

'Rim!' he gritted, at one point. 'When it says rim it means hit the rim – like that!'

Lily was doing her best, but soon got flustered.

'Never mind,' Lucy told her firmly, conscious that the poor woman was only trying to help out. 'If there's anything you can't manage, we'll miss it out. We won't need you in the carols. Just concentrate on that cymbal crash in "Tightrope Walker". That's the only really important bit for you. For the rest of it, just do what you can.'

The carols had gone well. Even Rachel had made a good job of her solo. Lucy had decided it would be easier to throw in a couple of piano solos of her own than to scout around twisting arms. Truth to tell, she had spent so much time trying to fill the corners of the band that she had let the guest spot slip her mind.

'I think I'm getting old,' she confided to Eileen.

'You wouldn't be normal if you weren't,' Eileen pointed out.

So Lucy slept fairly easy for the next two nights, thinking the worst crises were behind her.

Then at eleven o'clock on Friday evening her phone rang. Harry answered it, thinking it could only be someone from work for him. But it was Florence, for Lucy.

'We can't have the Spinners.'

'What?'

'We can't hold a concert at the Spinners. He told me tonight. He says he's had an official complaint.'

'An official complaint, Florrie? What does he mean? What official is this?'

'He says he's not licensed for public performances. Only for private wedding receptions. He says he faces prosecution if we go ahead.'

'Why didn't he tell us that before?'

'I think he didn't realise. I think somebody drew his attention to it – when they saw the posters, perhaps.'

'You mean, like, someone from Great Hulme Motors, for instance?'

'I wouldn't know. I feel really bad about this, Lucy.'

'Yes, well, I feel pretty bad too.'

'What are you going to do? Cancel?'

Lucy sighed and ran a hand over her forehead. She was in her nightie and had been just about to turn in with a good book while she waited for Harry to finish watching his TV programme.

'Unless I can think of any alternative.'

After a night of tossing and turning Lucy could think of three possible courses of action. She could cancel, she could find another venue – which would mean chasing up all the posters and changing them – or she could find a way round the legalities – like admitting the public free, for instance, and taking a collection.

She phoned the Spinners to make an appointment to speak to the manager. She had decided that this was the best way to prevent him from refusing to see her. If she just turned up without prior notice he might ask her to come back later when it was more convenient. But telephones have their disadvantages too. He insisted that he could not speak to her. Saturday was his busy day. Perhaps if she were to get in touch some time next week...

'But the concert is next week.'

'I've already told Florrie Robinson. You can't have the room. It's not licensed for public performance.'

'What if we don't charge admission?'

'Look – I've got a customer. I'll get back to you.' And he hung up.

Lucy saw her first pupil approaching. Saturday was her busy day as well.

By teatime he had not phoned.

'Shall you and me drop in at the Spinners for a drink, Harry?'

'It's a waste of time, love.' His voice was sympathetic, but quite firm. 'Most of his best customers play for t'Motors.'

Lucy sank into a chair. It had been a tiring day.

217

'What would you do, Harry, if you were me?'

'I'd cancel. It's just getting you down. You'll ruin your health if you go on like this.'

Yes, thought Lucy, but he's never been keen on the idea, anyway.

She spent an hour on the phone. Eileen said if she cancelled Tom would never let her forget it. Mary said if she cancelled she would understand, but please was there not some other way? Judith said that Wendy would be heartbroken if the concert did not take place. Ruth Anderton said if she were to cancel she would only be half the person she had thought she was.

Lucy was just checking out the phone number for Alice and Gladys when Sheena looked in to say she was not having any tea and would be getting some chips for herself and how was it going with the concert arrangements?

'I'm just phoning round to see how people feel about cancelling.'

'It's entirely up to you, Mrs B. But if it were me, I wouldn't let the buggers win.'

Lucy smiled wryly.

'I'll bear that in mind, Sheena.'

Then Harry took her out for a meal and tried to distract her from her worries by talking about a summer holiday and asking her opinion on different places to go: Isle of Man – Norfolk Broads – Inverness – how about Spain? Everybody was going to Spain these days. She only half took it in, but his own enthusiasm was well kindled. Spain had some good golf courses, apparently. He would get some brochures next week.

On Sunday morning, Lucy got the joint in the oven with a fair number of potatoes and Yorkshire pudding, adding a bread pudding well-dotted with sultanas and she and Harry set off to walk to the Morning Service. They usually attended Evensong, but she felt a particular urgency on this day. She could not wait to get down on her knees for a good pray.

There was a sharp frost decorating the blades of grass on the verges of the country lane. It turned hardy buttercup leaves into a vision of beauty. Their breath came out in clouds as they walked up the road together. The old bell tolled portentously, calling the faithful as in time immemorial. Lucy paused by the church hall which housed the Sunday school. It was a plain stone building with a slate roof which stood opposite the long gravel drive up to the church. It had a sprung wooden floor for dances and a proper stage and curtains you could draw. There were even a couple of small rooms side-stage which the Amateur Dramatic Society used as dressing rooms.

'Come on, love, we'll be late,' Harry urged

her, stamping his feet and blowing on his hands. He wished he had worn his gloves.

The bell fell silent as they pushed open the lychgate and crunched up the gravel path, past stones whose inscriptions could no longer be clearly read. The yew tree showered them with frost particles as a gust of wind stirred it and they were glad to hop into the porch. It was a small church, but drew a fair congregation from outside its boundaries, because it was prettier than the urban ones and its minister preached a mean sermon.

Lucy felt instantly better as she entered the shadowy interior, with its smell of Brasso and old wood, and its echoing organ chords. That was what being brought up to it did for you. It was like coming home, to come to church. You could tell God your troubles like you used to tell your dad when he was still alive. God didn't die. He was there same as always. How would this new generation manage without Him, that did not get brought up to believe in Him? Where would they turn for help? To a psychiatrist? To the Social Services? Alcohol? Television? Or was Sheena with her illegal substances just at the beginning of a trend? That was not a cheerful thought.

Anyway, when she had had a good pray and the time came to leave, she hung back, so that she could speak to the minister, without incurring impatient noises from the people behind. She had to find out if the church hall was free next Saturday.

It was! Of course he offered her the use of it for no fee. Though any donation to church funds would be appreciated.

'Any time you want a room to practise in,' he added, 'it's yours. As long as none of the regulars need it that evening, of course.'

So Lucy walked back home with a thankful heart. There were still all the posters to be altered, but they had the best part of a week to do that.

Next Wednesday, almost a complete band line-up gathered at Rivington Church Hall. It was no longer convenient for the Babylon Lane contingent, but at least everybody knew where it was. Also, though it did not boast a large car park, cars could be left in the road, because there was little traffic on a winter Wednesday night. Eileen brought the Hetherington girls, Lucy had gone out of her way to pick up Judith and Wendy. Florrie had given Winifred a lift. Joan and Deirdre had been dropped off by their husbands. Lily and her drum kit were transported by Jason and his friends. The euphonium player from the outskirts of Warrington who would share the baritone parts with Sheena, was not able to join them until Saturday. Finally Annette arrived with a twelve-year-old girl in possession of a soprano cornet.

'Ladies, this is Doreen,' Lucy informed them. 'She's come all the way from Wigan to play soprano cornet for us in the concert. She'll be staying with Annette till Sunday. We're very pleased to have you with us, Doreen. Would you like to sit next to Mrs Cashmore there, behind the top cornets?'

Judith pulled up a chair on her right and the girl sat there, not looking particularly nervous. It was all part of the kind of thing she was called upon to do. None of her friends would be there to laugh at her if she muffed a note. Moreover, Mrs Mackenzie had a super house and if her sons were a bit young, they did have all the latest records and a games room where they could play table tennis and snooker.

She was well able to cope with the carols, which she knew. She soon picked up 'The Old Castle' after hesitating over a couple of entries. She was going to be useful. Certainly she should have no difficulty with the solo in 'Scottish Airs', come next March.

Lily, however, was way out of her depth. They could not cut her out of the concert. It was too late. The damage could only be limited by asking her to play softly, except in 'Tightrope Walker', where her cymbal crash should point up the comic climax of Florrie's performance. If she could just do that, she would have filled her most important function.

During the interval Lucy found Eileen at her side.

'Do you want to know what I've found out?'

'Found out about what?'

'About Great Hulme Motors. It seems Alan Upton's dad plays for the Motors.'

'Alan Upton?'

'Him as got given Susie's bass at school.'

Lucy smiled.

'You know what this means.'

'Dirty work at the crossroads?'

'It means they're taking us seriously. It means they think we can beat them.' She emphasised the word 'beat' by slapping Eileen on the shoulder.

'Ouch!' said Eileen.

'That's the biggest compliment they could have paid us.' Lucy gazed around at her motley collection of musicians, with their assorted ages and backgrounds. 'All we have to do is realise their worst fears.'

Without exception her ladies had supported her in her decision not to cancel. Even Gladys, after expressions of indignation, had vowed that wild horses would not prevent her from taking part – even if they had to play in the street outside the Spinners – and serve 'em right.

So now this was Lucy's last chance to

mould them into shape before the concert. She pushed back her sleeves and grasped her baton.

'All right, everybody. In your places. There's no time to lose.'

Chapter 17

Concert day was windy and cold, but not wet. For the darkest time of the year that was quite good. Lucy spent the morning giving her piano pupils their last lesson before Christmas and the afternoon asking herself what she had forgotten. There was no question of eating any tea. She was up at the church hall by four o'clock, checking it was open, checking there were enough chairs, checking there were a couple of posters on the hall itself to draw the eye of passers-by and stamp upon the place its identity for anybody who may have been trying to find it.

She checked the piano. It was her first opportunity to do so. It was an upright, of course, with a beautiful rosewood veneer that had been well scuffed at the corners. As she suspected, the tone was very hard-edged, if not twangy. She played a few chords, experimenting with the pedals to see if she could ameliorate the sound. At least it played freely. She arpeggiated the length of the keyboard. Middle C had unpleasant overtones.

She hoped it would improve when the room was full of people. If they could fill the room with people. It was certainly very cold in there at the moment.

At five o'clock the caretaker arrived. He lit the coke boiler and began to carry the stacks of chairs out of the 'dressing rooms' and into the main body of the hall. Lucy purloined enough of them to set out on the stage for her players. As she did so she made a mental note to phone Annette to check that Maureen, the euphonium player from Warrington had arrived. It was a pity the girl had not had a chance to practise with them. But at least Lucy had heard her at the last festival and knew she was a good player. It was only a carol concert, after all.

She walked back home for a cup of tea and a bath. There was a feeling of snow in the air. Would they have a white Christmas? Would anybody turn up tonight? It did not have to be a full house. As long as there were enough people to give the band a feeling of playing to the public; enough to make the vicar feel his gesture had been worth making.

The vicar's wife acted as door person and took the money. She was an old hand at the business. The first members of the public to arrive were those who had brought band members with them. Winifred's daughter and son-in-law sat in the second row with her seven-year-old grandson, who kept bouncing up and down and asking loud questions. His first sweet was even now clattering around his teeth and the rest would be handed to him at judicious intervals.

Mr and Mrs Hetherington sat still as dummies right in the centre of the hall. He would travel miles to hear a good band and had a high standard to compare them with. But maybe he would make a willing suspension of criticism for an ensemble which included his daughters.

Harry and Tom went to down a last pint at the Bay Horse. They left Philip and Stuart to keep their places on the front mow. Two conspicuous mops of red hair. Close enough to distract Susie. Close enough to pull faces at Rebecca. Close enough to disconcert the whole band, should they decide to start falling about with laughter.

Old Bill was happy to sit at the back, next to Charity in her wheelchair, which was collapsible and could be brought in the van. Les and William joined them. The back of the hall was the best place to hear the trombones.

The band members crammed themselves into one of the small side rooms. There were enough cases to nearly fill one of those motorised trailers that carry passenger luggage to the hold of a plane. Space was in short supply.

'Susie can't find her music.'

'Surely you brought it with you, Susie?'

'It must be somewhere! Did you bring it with you?'

'I can't remember.'

After a panic, she found it in the car.

Wilfred came with his two daughters to sit in the front row, next but two to the Riley boys. Next to Harold and Christopher.

'Oh no!' breathed Lucy, as she craned around the door and spotted him, 'Whatever will he do this time?'

Even as she gazed, he dropped his paper programme on the floor and nearly fell off his chair picking it up again.

Alice sat in a corner of the side room, shaking quietly. She had a small bit of solo in 'The Old Castle' and could think of nothing else. Florrie was wrought up too, because Wilfred was there and she cared what he thought. But instead of going quiet like Alice, she became noisier than ever, pacing about the small space, bumping the bottoms of those who stooped to pick up their instruments.

'Have we got enough chairs on stage?' fretted Lucy. 'Have I counted right?'

'I'll check,' Judith said, glad to occupy her

mind. She was so petrified she felt sick. It was not the playing that worried her, it was being seen by a large number of people. She kept peering onto the stage to reassure herself that the repianos' seats were as well-concealed as possible.

Sheena and the Hetheringtons and Susie were already on stage, out of the way of the tiresome adults. The curtains were drawn, so it gave them an area to themselves. Maureen and Doreen, the two co-opted players, and Wendy had recently joined them.

'Who are all these people?' Rebecca wanted to know, thinking she was unobserved as she peeped round the curtains, when in fact half the audience could see her hand grasping the edge of the curtain.

'Mostly family, aren't they?' asked Doreen.

'They can't be. There's too many of them.'

It was true. The hall was filling up.

'Leave that curtain alone, Rebecca,' whispered Judith just before she returned to the dressing room to make a last visit to the toilet. 'The audience can see you.'

Rebecca made a show of obedience by letting it go. Rachel took her place.

'There's Ruth Anderton just arrived. Her girlfriend's with her!'

'Let's have a look!'

They stood there giggling. Wendy frowned. She could not understand their mirth.

'She has girls like the rest of us have boys,'

Sheena explained to her, quite kindly.

'Oh really?' Wendy tried to look as if she understood what that meant. 'I didn't know you could.'

'Well don't start getting ideas,' Rachel told her nastily.

'Let's have a look!' Susie pushed Rachel aside and grabbed the edge of the curtain. The audience was already beginning to enjoy the entertainment. 'Holy smoke! There's Mr Greenhalgh!'

'What?'

'No it isn't. Yes it is. No it isn't – wait. Yes it is!'

'Will you people get away from that curtain?' rang out Lucy's voice angrily from behind them. 'Everybody can see you. It looks very, very bad. I don't want to have to tell you again.'

They slunk into their chairs and fiddled with their music, heads buzzing with excitement.

Lucy called the rest of her musicians onto the stage. It would keep the young people in order to have everybody there. Time was pressing, anyway. The vicar was here now, asking Lucy to let him know if she wanted him to go on stage and say a few words.

'Can you put out the hall lights when I give the signal?'

'Wouldn't you like a glowing introduction?'

'We'd prefer it if you said a few words afterwards.'

A glowing introduction was the last thing she wanted. She knew the vicar and his glowing introductions.

'Who's going to do the curtains?'

'Mr Robinson volunteered.'

Oh no! Anybody but Wilfred!

Too late.

The lights were switched out, row by overhead row, and in the hush of expectation that followed, the band struck up behind the curtains with 'Hark! The Herald Angels Sing'. Wilfred was supposed to open them at once, but there were crossed wires somewhere and it was the end of the first verse before the beige-coloured drapes began to move. Then they became stuck half way and his efforts to shift them could be noted in a series of little twitches. They only whooshed fully open by the end of the second verse, to reveal Doreen, the soprano cornet player on the one extreme and the trombonists on the other, to their anxious relatives.

With the sudden freeing of the curtain, Wilfred fell over backwards, letting go of the cord he had been tugging. Of course, the curtains began to close again of their own accord. He made a noisy dive for the moving toggle, which everybody could hear and which made bulges in the curtain whose activities the audience could watch. He succeeded in arresting their progress at the half-way stage, hauled them jerkily fully open and attached the cord this time onto some hooks he found on the wall behind him.

By now the closing chords were sounding, so he decided to return to his seat, not via the dressing room, but over the apron in full view of the audience. Lucy watched him pointedly as he jumped down.

'Thank you very much for your excellent work,' she told him in the brief silence that fell. 'We'll phone you if we need you again,' thereby giving the audience a chance to let out the roar of laughter they had been holding back for some time.

The band played another carol and then it was the turn of the 'Medley of Scottish Airs'. Ruth Anderton made magnificent work of her cadenza, but refrained from prolonging it, knowing that Mary's was to follow. They played 'Silent Night' and although Rachel sounded nervous, she got through it without falling apart. Then it was time for a guest solo.

Lucy had to leave the stage and reappear through the side door to where the rosewood piano of dubious provenance stood near one side of the apron. Plunging boldly into Chopin's Waltz in D flat major, she discovered to her horror that middle G was sticking. It had not happened when she had tried out the piano earlier. She could only assume that it was a result of the room warming up. This being one note in a rapidly reiterated group of four, it made quite a difference to a tune with which most of the audience would surely be familiar.

Gritting her teeth, she put the right hand up an octave, only to encounter a whole array of sticking notes. The perspiration was beading her brow and her heart was beating dangerously. Wishing she had had the nerve to abandon it at the start, she brought it instead to a premature close with a gap-toothed downward run and a thunderous chord in the safe area at the top of the bass clef, making it sound as though she had strayed into a piece of Beethoven by mistake. That was Chopin's thirty-three-second Minute Waltz. Sorry, Chopin.

Everybody applauded politely, but Lucy would like to have taken an axe to the piano. She could see Harry and Tom and the Riley boys with shoulders shaking in the front row and she knew that it was unlikely that she would ever be allowed to forget Chopin and the Sunday school piano.

They continued with more carols, including one the audience were supposed to join in on, but could not be heard to do so, though lips here and there were seen to move. Then the trombones put a strong finish on the first half of the programme with 'We Three Kings' before the band retired to the dressing room, leaving the curtains open, at Lucy's insistence.

There were no stiff whiskies to be had in the interval, only cups of tea. Lucy forestalled any mention of Chopin by asking Harry to fetch her one. Then she sought out Ruth.

'The piano's a disaster!'

'I rather gathered that.'

Ruth's suppressed smile was more irritating than outright laughter would have been.

'What can we do for the second half. Any ideas?'

'My guitar's in the car, but it has to have an amplifier.'

'There's one in the other side room. Shall I ask to borrow it?'

'Don't ask. Just get it. Get a microphone too if there is one.'

When Harry returned with a cup of lukewarm tea, Lucy drew a grateful draught and begged him to get Tom and transfer that little old amplifier in the side room to just below the apron of the stage. What if it did not work? Against Ruth's advice, she asked the vicar about it. It belonged to the Youth Club, but he was sure they would not mind it being used provided it was properly taken care of.

Most of the band members spent the interval with their relatives. Judith stayed holed up in the dressing room. Joan and Deirdre got themselves some refreshments and came to join her. The younger ones wandered in and out, having to be told over and over again to shut the door. As soon as Eileen realised that Joe Greenhalgh was there, Susie having drawn her attention to him in a loud voice, her one thought was to keep Judith from finding out.

'Tell everybody not to say anything about it, will you? Not till afterwards, at any rate.'

'Wendy knows.'

'Somehow I think Wendy will keep her mouth shut. Where is Mrs Cashmore, anyway?'

'She stayed in the dressing room.'

'Good.'

Eileen made her way there, but she was too late. Rachel had got there first.

Judith was sitting on the steps to the stage having her head held between her knees by Joan. Deirdre stood by, a saucepan at the ready.

'What happened?'

Judith raised her head. Her face was grey.

'I thought she was going to faint,' Joan told her.

'I didn't think it would upset her,' protested Rachel, not quite concealing her glee. 'I just thought she would want to know.'

'Go and get a drink of water,' Eileen snapped at her, longing to give her a clout on the ear. 'Quickly.'

When Lucy joined them she could see that Judith was going to be of no use for the second half.

'Can you play the rep part on your own?' she asked Deirdre.

'Sure,' said Deirdre, unabashed.

'Everybody on stage,' Lucy ordered them. 'The curtains are open, so I want you to file on in the order you sit, far-stage persons first. When the audience sees you, they will all sit down and become quiet. If they don't, we'll give them a burst of "O Come, All Ye Faithful".' She held Susie back. 'Go and fetch Mr Greenhalgh.'

She was taking a chance, but she hated to see Judith suffering like this, she hated to leave her alone in the side room. If her instincts were right, this might give her stricken repiano player the boost which was long overdue. She hoped her instincts were right.

'And hurry!'

By the time Susie returned with him, the promised quiet was indeed beginning to settle and the vicar rushed to dim the lights.

'Good girl,' Lucy commended her. 'Now get on stage.'

Susie clambered up the stage steps. Lucy caught the eye of the gentleman who was standing looking rather helpless in the doorway. She gestured him towards Judith.

Then she had to go on stage herself.

Everybody was playing well. Whatever else was going wrong all around her, Lucy was pleased with her band. Wendy did a great job on 'O Little Town of Bethlehem', in spite of her fears for her mother. 'The Old Castle' passed without spookery. When the time came for the guest spot, Lucy gave the signal to Ruth, who left the stage by the other side room door so that she could grab her guitar and make a theatrical entrance.

'And now, ladies and gentlemen,' Lucy addressed the audience, her baton clasped in both hands, 'we have a special guest who has kindly consented to appear at short notice. She has taken time off from her busy schedule to be with us tonight and she's none other than Ruth Anderton...' she put out a hand to give Ruth the cue to enter and the audience to applaud, both of which occurred, '...of that popular and well-known group...' she paused, then turned to Ruth. 'What's its name?'

'The Stonemasons,' Ruth told her crisply.

Ruth tapped the hurriedly set-up microphone. It was dead. Brilliant! She knelt on the apron and leaned over to examine the amplifier. She found herself looking straight into the grey eyes of Harold Mackenzie. Mentally she checked her cleavage. Thank goodness she was in a demure blouse and not one of the low-cut tops she had to wear at the Granary. A small boy sat there too.

'Hey sonny, what's your name?'

'Christopher.'

'Right, Christopher, will you follow that flex to the wall and switch on anything you find down there for me, please?'

He did so. There was an ear-destroying howl from the microphone. She quickly clicked off the two-way switch under its head.

'See that knob, Christopher – no, that one. Just turn it anti-clockwise a little.'

He stood scratching his head while he worked out which way round the figures went on a clock's face. He turned to look at the clock at the back of the hall. The audience laughed.

'This way?'

'That's it.'

He turned it, she angled the mike head and switched it on. It was fine.

'Take a gold star, Christopher,' she told him.

'Where to?'

The audience roared in delight.

'I think you should be up here,' she told him. 'But not tonight. This is *our* show.'

Harold made him sit down.

She addressed the audience, having to bend a little because the mike was too low, but she did not dare tempt fate by adjusting it.

'That was my first number, entitled "An Electronic Hangover". I'm not really a vocalist and the guitar is not my instrument, but nevertheless you'll be pleased to know that I'm going to accompany myself in a couple of Doris Day numbers, beginning with "Que Sera Sera". If you want to, please join in.' She twanged a couple of strings and tuned them by twisting the pegs at the top of the fingerboard.

'Look at it this way,' she added. 'You can drown me out if you sing loudly enough.'

So she gave voice to a couple of popular songs and since they were in good tune and well-liked and the audience was in a good mood, they went down fine. There was even a call for an encore, and it did not come from Sarah.

Following on such gaiety with a sacred hymn was a daunting task for the most seasoned of performers, but Mary proved herself a worthy Ainscough. She made her unaccompanied opening to 'Once in Royal David's City' quite strongly, but softly enough for the audience to fall quiet the better to hear her. The mood was transformed by the time the band crept in with the accompaniment in verse two. Afterwards, there was a respectful pause before the applause burst forth.

Then another turnaround of mood. It was time for 'Tightrope Walker'. Florrie brought her music stand to the apron, just off centre stage so she could stand at an angle, facing away from Wilfred. In fact she knew it by heart, but felt it was wiser to have her music there, just in case.

It could not be said that the backing was perfect, but nobody noticed, because Florrie had them mesmerised with her highly individualistic approach. They never knew what she was going to do next. Neither did Lucy. Florrie in front of an audience was a different person. On a knife-edge – or in this case a tightrope – Lucy kept the band with the soloist, through all her various turns of speed. Florrie added an unscheduled tremolo which expanded into a see-sawing glissando then stopped. Florrie took the trombone from her mouth and looked down at her feet, as at a fallen circus performer. She looked at the audience and shook her head sadly, then ripped into the end of the cadenza at top speed, while Lucy dragged the band with her right up to the climactic cymbal crash. Lily, shaking, had been waiting for this moment all evening. She raised her stick as high as she could, but, since she was crammed right up against the side wall, it caught in the curtain, so that when she brought her hand down with all her might, there was nothing in it and all the people heard was the noise of a stick clattering to the floor.

The band filled in the closing chords and that was the end of the show. From somewhere a bouquet of flowers appeared and was presented to Lucy. The vicar gave them a glowing epilogue and people filed out into the chill December night.

The sky was full of stars. There would be a hard frost in the morning.

Chapter 18

'Anybody want to come back to my place for drinks?' Annette sang out over the figures who were trying to find their instrument cases all at the same time in the confined space of the little side-stage dressing room. It was essential to catch them before they all left. 'It's not far to walk if you haven't got a lift,' she added. 'Just down the road and turn right past the reservoir.'

'What about the instruments?'

'Perhaps those with cars can find room in the boot?'

'What about your van, Alice?' Lucy asked helpfully.

'I can't go. Charrers and Dad need taking home.'

'They can come too if they like.'

'Dad wouldn't. But thanks for the offer.'

Alice would like to have gone and so would Charity, she was sure, but to take old Bill would be to cast an air of gloom over the happy throng.

Wendy stood looking lost.

'Where's your mum?' asked Eileen.

'I don't know.'

'She asked me to tell you she's waiting in the white sports car outside.' Joan smiled kindly at the little girl. 'She said she wants you to go and join her there.'

Wendy's face fell. She knew who had a white sports car. She did not want to go.

'Come on,' Eileen held out her hand. 'I'll take you.'

Lucy had remembered to have some flowers put by to give to Annette as a thanks for the hospitality she had provided to the players from Wigan and Warrington. She had also got chocolates for Doreen and Maureen to thank them for helping out. Now she had it in mind to give the bouquet which she herself had been presented with to Ruth for stepping in and saving her bacon when the chips were down.

But Ruth and Sarah had left instantly for the Granary and were already in the Hillman, bouncing up the rutted road to the converted dance hall. The Stonemasons would be well into their first session by the time they arrived.

Les could see that Mary wanted to stay for the party, but taking William was out of the question at that time of night.

'Let me drop you off,' he urged her. 'You can get Flo and Wilfred to run you home.'

'But William won't go to sleep if I'm not there. Anyway, you've had him all evening.'

'He's my son,' Les pointed out, 'and he's practically asleep now.'

It was true, William sat in the back with one arm round the euphonium, his eyes unfocused but quite content.

'Did you enjoy the concert, you two?' Alice wanted to know as the Hot Stompers' van chugged noisily through Major Bottoms. She knew there would be no flattery from either of them, which made their opinions all the more valuable.

'Trombones were grand,' Bill told her, 'but they should face outwards not sideways. I thought you were going to stay behind that curtain all evening.'

'Oh that was Wilfred. What can you expect?'

'That girl was excellent,' Charity put in. 'The one who did the songs with the guitar. Really professional. Where did you find her?'

'She found us.'

'That was lucky, then.'

'Oh aye. It was lucky all reet.'

242

Her tone of voice left the word 'but' hovering unsaid. Charity did not press her to explain. She realised that if Alice had wanted to divulge anything she would have done so. She would get it out of her when their dad was not listening.

'If you want to know what was wrong...' Bill continued, as one about to reach the best part.

'Hey up – here he goes!' said Alice, slowing down to take the left-hand turn at the Bay Horse.

'...there were not enough bass. That trumpet wants swapping for a cornet and your percussionist should be in Billy Smart's circus.'

'Did you not like our Mary's solo?'

Alice felt he really ought to say something about it. 'Oh that. Aye. It were all reet – for a euph.'

The white sports car pulled up outside Judith's new house. She and Wendy almost fell out, like items only held in place by the shut door.

'Thank you, Joe,' said Judith, but she did not sound happy.

'I'll be in touch,' he called in a subdued voice and drove away.

'Are you all right, Mummy?'

They were the first words Wendy had spoken since leaving the hall.

Judith turned the key in the lock and pushed open the door.

'I'm all right love. A cup of tea would be nice.'

'I'll make it.'

Wendy scuttled off to the kitchen and Judith decided that this time she must put her daughter in the picture and not leave her to find things out from other people. She had been a cowardly mother. She had always avoided difficult issues. Wendy was young, but she was mature enough to be told.

'Mr Greenhalgh is getting a divorce.'

'Oh.'

'His wife is divorcing him. She is going to say it's because of me.'

'Is she mad at you?'

'It doesn't matter whether she is or not. What matters is it may get into the papers.'

Wendy stood with the tea caddy in her hands. The kettle sang.

'They'll know at St Hilda's.'

'Probably.'

'Does that mean we'll have to leave?'

'I hope not.'

Gladys was also to be brought back by Wilfred and Florence, for whom the night had hardly started, they were so keen to continue enjoying themselves. There were pink patches of colour in Florence's cheeks and she could not stop talking. Mary and Gladys wandered from room to room admiring the curtains and the carpets and the tasteful pictures and table lamps.

The kitchen was spacious and spotless. Its walls were covered in useful cupboards. The cooker had two ovens as well as a grill and an extractor hood over it. There was even an electric tin-opener on the wall. Everything a person could possibly want.

Lucy had only intended to stay at Annette's for half an hour or so. She had gone along mainly because Sheena was keen and she thought it would be nice to take her where she would be out of harm's way for one Saturday, at least. But Harry hung on. Tom was there and several other men. The hostess was a treat for the eyes and the drink was flowing freely, so as far as he was concerned this was the best part of the evening.

'How did things go with Judith?' Eileen asked Lucy.

'I don't know,' Lucy told her. Her headache was a thing of the past after the tablets which Annette had given her and which she had washed down with a whisky and lemonade. She felt rather light-headed, but perfectly capable, thank you. 'I think I'll phone her tomorrow morning and find out.'

'Phone me will you, when you've phoned her?'

'Yes, but don't you go talking to Tom

245

about it.'

'In that case, you'll have to keep it from Harry, won't you?'

'Gossipy creatures, men, aren't they?'

The schools broke up. The pupils of St Hilda's assembled for the last time that year. Wendy sat in one of the rows of younger girls, most of whom were trying to look interested in what was going on when in reality they were thinking about the Christmas presents to come. Wendy turned to her new friend Jenny.

'Do you like being at St Hilda's?'

'Of course. Don't you?'

'Oh yes,' she said wistfully. 'Very much.'

Christmas came and went. Almost before they knew it, another year had begun. Lucy decided she really had to get down to work now. This was the final straight before the winning post. She knew that such band members as she had could play well enough together. The tuning was quite good now. The boy who had got himself put on Susie's bass had done them all a favour in the end. They had had a good audience for their concert, who had seemed to enjoy themselves. They had even taken quite a bit at the door. Lucy had it in mind to give some of the takings to the church, since the vicar had been such a friend in need. She would consult Mary, or maybe put it to the rest of the band. They would surely agree.

Meanwhile she had had the problem of the percussion thrown right back in her lap. Lily had phoned to say she did not want to play drums again. Lucy thanked her profusely for helping them out but did not try to get her to change her mind.

Judith had acquired a new serenity. Joe Greenhalgh had told her that after the divorce he would like to continue to see her. He was sorry about what had happened but they had both suffered the consequences and was there any chance they could start going out together again once the dust had settled?

So unexpectedly Judith had been given the opportunity to right the wrong she had done to her conscience and thereby to her self-respect. She clasped her resolve around her and told him that she would not see him again until the divorce was through and he was a free man. After that – it was up to him, if he still wanted her. Her guilt fell off her like the albatross from the ancient mariner's neck. Suddenly she could live with herself again.

There was a good turnout when the band met again in January. They had all enjoyed themselves so much at the concert that they could not wait to get back into harness.

Those who had difficulty travelling to Rivington made their own arrangements for transport. Lucy did not have to worry her head planning for them. What a luxury!

Florrie crashed in, humming a tune.

'Happy Christmas!' Eileen greeted her, holding out a mouthpiece-shaped package wrapped in bright holly-patterned paper.

'You didn't have to do that, Eileen,' protested Florrie.

'Open it.'

Florrie opened it; it was the old silver bass trombone mouthpiece.

'It spent some weeks in the canal,' Eileen explained, 'But we cleaned it out and we let it soak overnight in Dettol.'

Lucy came up.

'That's never the same one that got thrown in t'canal, is it?'

'Unless there's a few of them down there.'

'How did you get it? Did someone give Tom a diver's suit for Christmas?'

'Stuart and Philip. Would you believe it? They made a raft out of packing cases and got out on the water. Took the garden rake and tied a stick to the handle. They were out there the best part of an afternoon, scraping about. You wouldn't believe the rubbish they dredged up. Silly monkeys. They'd have caught their death if they'd fallen in. It were freezing at the time.'

'You must let me give them something for

their trouble,' offered Florrie, none too eagerly.

'No need. They came across a whole horde of silver cutlery down there. And a gold bracelet. Stolen, apparently. The police say there might be a reward.'

'Well,' said Lucy. 'Some good came out of it, then.'

Once again, she reflected, an attempt at sabotage had turned out to their advantage. Perhaps enemy action was nothing to be feared if it resulted in benefits like this.

'I see you've brought Rachel and Rebecca again,' Lucy remarked to Eileen.

'It's the obvious thing to do, isn't it?'

'Do I take it that there's no bad feeling any more – between your families, I mean?'

'There never was anything serious, as far as Tom and I were concerned. It was just children being children. But you know what Mr H is like. That family is so straight-laced.'

'So...' Lucy was more intrigued than ever. But there was no time to follow it up. '...you must tell me all about it afterwards.'

'But there's nothing...'

Lucy interrupted her by raising her voice and telling them all to get seated and to put up the 'Prelude to a Storm', because this was going to be the Prelude to some Really Hard Work. She meant it. Instead of giving the good players a satisfying run, as at most practices, she concentrated on the less experienced and the lazy. If anybody fluffed any notes, she made them take the phrase over and over again by themselves with all their colleagues listening. It made it enjoyable for nobody, but it concentrated their minds wonderfully. Sloppiness disappeared.

Each section had the complicated rhythmic phrasing in turn. She ran them through it group by group. The tenor horns were working in rather a lot of sharps, but it was not a problem as long as they went over it often enough to get thoroughly accustomed to the fingering, so that they did not have to work it out each time.

At the halfway break she called together her 'consultative committee' of Florence, Judith and Ruth. Now that they were in Rivington Church Hall, they were able to retire to a side room, stacked chairs permitting.

'I'd like you to give me any comments you may have heard about the concert, good or bad,' she told them.

'Dad says not enough bass,' Florrie told her. 'And the drums were a non-starter.'

'I think that goes without saying. Anybody any solutions?'

There was silence.

'Advertise,' suggested Ruth, trying to perch on a stack of three chairs. 'You never know who's out there.' The chairs wobbled.

She pulled one off and sat on that.

'We did that a while back. I suppose we could try again.'

'Do all the papers,' Ruth advised. 'Not just the *Chorley Guardian*, but the *Horwich Journal, Bolton Evening News, Darwen Times* – anywhere.'

'Is there a *Darwen Times?*'

'Probably not, but you know what I mean.'

'Is there nobody at all at St Hilda's, Judith? Surely you've got a school band.'

'We have a chamber orchestra. There's a French horn player who isn't very good but no other brass and there certainly isn't a set of drums. They don't consider brass and drums very lady-like, I'm afraid. And it is a school for young ladies. We have a couple of timps and a triangle. That's all.'

They started up the practice again and put in some more time on 'Scottish Airs', to attend to a few problems which had become apparent only at the concert. Then they finished with 'Regimental Selection' just to give Ruth and Florence the chance to let rip.

Eileen helped Lucy put the chairs away afterwards. It was much colder in the hall and the sound reverberated a bit, but they were still grateful to be there.

'Susie's doing well,' Lucy commended Eileen. 'To say she hasn't been playing very long, she's making great progress. We won't regret buying that bass, I'm sure of it.'

'If it didn't work out we could sell it,' Eileen told her. 'Tom says you can always sell a good one. But it's nice to hear you say she's doing all right,' Eileen thanked her. 'She's really keen. She's taken to it very well. I'm pleased. I could have done without that Maureen girl and her comments, though.'

'What comments?' Lucy was surprised. She had heard nothing.

'About it being such a baby bass. I don't think she meant it unkindly,' she hastened to add, 'but it really upset Susie.'

'Baby bass? Whatever did she mean?'

'Her dad plays one of those thumping great double B flat basses. She just thought the E flat looked small. She wanted to blow it. You know how thoughtless young people can be.'

'Tell Susie not to take any notice. She's doing grand. Tell her you're proud of her, and tell her so am I.'

It was not until she was lying in bed, trying to drop off to sleep against the sound of Sheena's radio, that the significance of what Eileen had said suddenly hit her. She sat bolt upright.

'B flat bass!' she cried, like some Archimedes rising from the bath.

'Have you gone mad?' Harry wanted to

know, reaching out a hand for the bedside clock to see what time it was.

'Maureen's dad has got a double B flat bass. That's what Eileen said.'

'For crying out loud – literally!'

Lucy sank back onto the pillow and said no more, but she was going to be spending some time on that phone again this week-end.

Chapter 19

Lucy ascertained that Maureen's dad would be at the festival, blowing his double B flat bass for his local band. She checked that he did not object to his daughter using it too. It was a piece of real good fortune. The girl was quite accustomed to blowing it and though it was not her favourite instrument, it did not have anything as difficult written for it as she would have had to play on baritone.

But, of course, this put extra responsibility onto Sheena. Now that Maureen was no longer playing alongside her, she would be unable to pass on anything she could not manage to somebody else. Lucy went out and bought a book of exercises for brass instruments and gave it to her.

'You could be a good player if you worked a bit more,' she told her, to sweeten the pill. 'I'd consider it a real favour if you'd spend an hour a day on some of these exercises.'

'But I'm working all day, Mrs B.'

'Can you fit it in in the early evening, perhaps?'

Sheena took the book.

'Anything to please you,' she said

She half meant it. As she had drifted from room to room at Annette's house after the concert the thought had occurred to her that, were it not for the band, the only way she was likely to find herself in such a swanky house was by breaking into it. There were some nice items worth nicking, too. A crystal ashtray, for instance, which she had picked up and almost caught herself slipping it into her pocket, before pulling herself together and reminding herself of the bath salts Annette had brought her while she was remanded in custody.

It was beginning to occur to her that she could be on a par with the others. She could feel proud to be there legitimately. She could feel respectable. She began to sense that there were better things than tawdry loot. When she was playing in the concert, up there on stage, she felt as good as any of the others. (Except Big Flo and Bent Ruth, of course.) She did not want to lose that feeling. She would practise the baritone every day. If she remembered to.

On Wednesday Lucy asked Judith whether the girl who played the French horn for St Hilda's chamber orchestra might consider playing tenor for them.

'I doubt it. As far as I know the fingering is different. Anyway, she's not very good. She makes some untidy entries.'

'It's only for the third tenor. She wouldn't have to be good. Just able to read.'

'I'll mention it to her. But what about an instrument?'

'I don't know. Any chance you could borrow one from the Salvation Army?'

'I'll ask,' Judith promised, though she did not relish getting her begging bowl out again. 'Did you have any luck with the adverts?'

'They've only just gone in. I haven't any high hopes. We've already scraped that particular barrel rather dry – no offence to our much-valued advert-answerers, of course.'

Next she drew Ruth aside.

'What's the difference between playing a trumpet and playing a cornet?'

'Practically none. The cornet mouthpiece is usually deeper and rounder. That's all.'

'So if I asked Annette to change to a cornet for the concert would she still be able to play?'

'She might crack a few top notes. It takes months to get accustomed to a mouthpiece.

But I'm taking the most difficult bits. I expect she would be able to play most of the stuff she's got without trouble.'

'Would she be upset if I asked her to change, do you think?'

'Am I my sister's keeper, Lucy? It would be a courtesy to give her some time to try it out, I can say that much. As to her reaction – well, she's playing a better instrument than you're likely to be able to find for her.'

She turned away, reluctant to be implicated.

Lucy did not find that answer very reassuring, but she went ahead and put it to Annette.

'Now personally I like the trumpet,' she added, 'and I like the sound that you make with yours. But I've been told that an adjudicator is likely to pick on it and take marks off because it's not strictly authentic for a brass band.'

'So,' Annette broke in, to hurry her to the point, 'Do you want me to stay away, or buy a cornet, or what?'

She sounded irritable. After all she had done for the band, this did not feel like gratitude.

'Oh no. I'll borrow a cornet you can use. Just for the festival. I'll be happy to have you play trumpet again afterwards.'

Alf and Bill sat either side of the fireplace on

a raw February afternoon.

'Tha's a bit quiet this afty, Bill.'

Bill grunted. His arthritis was always at its worst at this time of year. His elbows were giving him gyp and his knuckles were not far behind in the agony stakes. This destroyed his pleasure in cigarettes. He would have given up smoking, but what would he have left if he did?

'Tha'll have summat to complain about thissen,' Bill told him, 'when my daughters play in t'Brass Festival. Did you go to t'concert?'

'I thought it were cancelled.'

'You mean you hoped it were. They held it at Rivington.'

'It's like the inside of a tin drum there.'

'Not when it's full of people, it isn't. And it were full of people.'

'They must have had some fellers – to help them out.'

'Nope. All ladies. And girls.'

'Some good-lookers, were there?'

'One or two. But they sounded all right. Aye. They were all reet. Need a few things changing here and there.'

'I heard they'd got one or two smashers in the front row. Hoping to catch the judge's eye, I bet. Bit of leg here and there.'

'Well they're a lot prettier than your lot, needless to say, but they're more than that. Believe me Alf, with a new drummer and a bit more weight on the lower end they'll be making your lot sound like a herd of elephants looking for a lost waterhole.'

'There's a bed-sit going vacant at the Ridgeway, Mrs B,' Sheena came out with while they were doing the evening dishes. 'I'd like to take it, if it's all right with you. It's only just round the corner from work.'

'It's all right with me, Sheena. I'll have to notify the authorities. How soon would you want to move?'

'Next Sunday.'

'Why don't you stay here till after the festival. It's only a week.'

'Why? Does it make any difference?'

'I suppose not.'

Lucy had misgivings, but she could not put them into words. It would sound as if she did not trust her out of her sight. Which, alas, she did not.

She and Harry ferried Sheena's few belongings down to the Adlington flat the following Sunday. Really Sheena had so little it was rather sad. The flat was fully furnished and had cutlery and pans and all the cooking and eating paraphernalia, but the kitchen was about the size of most people's toilets – just a primitive sink with a tap that dripped and a greasy gas cooker with one hob. There was ill-fitting lino on the floor and patches of damp on the walls. Sheena was pleased with it. It was her first home.

Lucy ransacked her own linen cupboard and found her a nice warm candlewick bedspread.

'And don't be afraid to ask for any help if you need it.'

'I'll be all right.'

There was no telephone and the bathroom was shared, but what did you expect for seventeen and sixpence a week?

Once that little matter was attended to, Lucy phoned Florrie to ask if she had any ideas about where to find a spare cornet. After some thought, Florrie suggested they could use some of the money they had collected when they had gone playing carols, if they still had it.

'I think Mary put it in the bank with Harold Mackenzie's loan,' Lucy told her. 'But we ought to check with Eddie Picker-skill.'

'Mary's the one to get in touch with him, if she will. He seemed to have a soft spot for her. Leave it with me and I'll let you know before Wednesday.'

The news was good, from that quarter. As they assembled at Rivington Church Hall on the Wednesday, Lucy had high hopes that the biggest problems were behind them.

'Did you have any luck with the adverts?' Ruth wanted to know, as she unpacked her

Westminster and jiggled its valves.

'There were no brass players.'

'None at all?'

'Not one. But never mind. I've been given the name of a drummer. They said she was called Jean Cooper. Do you know her?'

Ruth shook her head.

'They said she would try to get here last week,' added Lucy, 'but not to worry if she couldn't make it, because she would be here the following week. That's tonight and there's no sign of her. If she doesn't turn up I don't know what I'm going to do.'

'Did you get her phone number?'

'Yes. I've got it here somewhere.'

'You're sure it was Jean Cooper and not Gene Krupa?'

Lucy went pale.

'Oh no – I – I'm sure – I'm positive it was...' Her voice tapered away. Plainly, she was less than positive

'If she isn't here by the break, I think you ought to try to phone her then,' Ruth advised her gently.

Most of the players had arrived, including a girl called Penny, who had come with Judith. She had agreed to try the tenor horn and had surprised them all by playing very well. She told them that it was kid's stuff after the French horn and she liked it so much that she was not going to want to give it up again afterwards. Judith had written the fingering in above those notes in the relevant horn parts where they differed from horn in F. She had then given them to Penny, who discovered that the instrument was far more lip-friendly than the French horn, which had a tiny mouthpiece and a habit of slipping off the notes like a live fish off a plate. She had had trouble with top Fs and Gs on the French horn, but found she could play up to top C on the tenor.

Joan and Deirdre were the only ones not coming, but Lucy knew she could rely on them for the festival. She waited until those present were all seated, then she addressed them.

'If I call an extra practice on Friday, how many of you couldn't make it?'

Nobody spoke up, though a few of them knew they would have to make special arrangements.

'I do feel it's crucial to have one practice with our soprano and double bass, and also with the percussionist in case she fails to turn up again this evening.'

They did some work on the by-now-familiar 'Scottish Airs' and laboured over a 'Prelude' in which most of the special effects were missing. The time for packing up arrived and no Jean Cooper had gladdened their hearts with an appearance.

'Is there a phone here?' Ruth asked Lucy.

'I'll go home. It's not far. Tell everybody I

won't be long.' She rushed home to her telephone and dialled the number. For a long time there was no reply. She was about to give up when somebody picked up the receiver.

'Can I speak to Jean, please?' asked Lucy.

'Who?'

'Is Jean Cooper there?'

'I'm afraid you've got the wrong number. This is a Masonic Lodge and we're supposed to be ex-directory.'

Ruth could tell as soon as she returned what had happened.

'It was a hoax, wasn't it?'

'How did you know?'

'I didn't know it was, I just feared it was.'

'But it's wasted so much precious time. How can I find someone now? It's too late. Just look at all the people who are going to be let down. What about the van for the handicapped? How can anybody find that funny? I don't find it funny at all.'

'Let's split the problem. If you can have a set of drums here on Friday, I'll have someone here to play them.'

'There's a set of drums in the side room, along with the amplifier.'

'The Youth Club, no doubt.'

'I'll ask the vicar.'

So on Friday they had a fuller band than they had ever had before. Not only soprano this time, but a big beefy double B flat bass and a full row of tenors – three of them. As soon as Sheena came and the drummer, she would at last be able to hear them as they would sound at the festival.

The trombones were there and warming up, topped by a strong cornet section, complete with Annette. Eddie Pickerskill had offered them the loan of his own beloved cornet – the one with which he had taken so many solos in the old days.

'Only you must promise to play it real champion.'

'You can be sure of that.'

He never touched it now. He was going to look forward to hearing it again at the festival, along with all the others in this ladies' band.

It felt wrong to Annette. It sounded wrong when she blew it, like a trumpet with a North Country accent. Ungraciously, perhaps, she was glad she was only expected to use it for a short time.

At last Ruth came through the door, trailing a tall, thin girl with short wavy hair and rather soulful eyes.

'This is Trish, Lucy. Have you got the drums set up?'

'Yes, they're over here.'

Trish approached them. Nervousness was stamped all over her.

'Go on!' Ruth urged her. 'Knock 'em cold.'

Trish sat down and ran her sticks over the assortment of drums in front of her with rather bony hands. She adjusted here and there, raised her seat, hit the cymbal to check it out, then sat and waited, pushing back her hair self-consciously. She obviously knew her stuff.

'Ruth is here, ladies, so let's all tune in to her cornet, please,' announced Lucy. Sheena had still not arrived. Lucy wished she had made her postpone her move until after the festival. She no longer had any control over her arrival time. But it would have been un-fair to Harry to keep her for an extra week, when he was so desperate for her to go.

They tuned up carefully, paying particular attention to the basses. One of the things Lucy had noticed about the less highly placed bands in last year's festival was that when basses were out of tune with one another you could hear a pulsing beat which nothing could hide.

She asked them to put up 'Scottish Airs', just to let Trish in lightly. There was a bit of cymbal and wood-block in that piece, but not too much of anything going on at once. The girl played well. No hesitations, no mistiming – what a treat! Her snare drum work in the 'Road to the Isles' was a bit too loud. Lucy asked her to tone it down and immediately she toned it down.

Break time came and no Sheena. Lucy

began to worry. Her part was important. There should really have been two baritones and now there were none. She had already shared out among the trombones as much second baritone as she could. She would have to drive down to the Ridgeway and see her after the practice. Somebody would have to give her a lift in tomorrow. Eileen had a full car load. So did Annette. Judith had no car. The Ainscoughs and their van, that was the answer.

After the break they took on the acid test of the 'Prelude to a Storm', which of course employed every bit of the percussion from temple-block to bass drum. There was a cymbal crescendo roll and various runs across the different sizes of tam-tam to give the impression of meteorological pyro-technics. She could tell that Trish did not get it all quite right, but then she was sight-reading. She played it twice as well second time through. What a find!

'Where did you find her?' she asked Ruth as they were packing up the kit afterwards. 'She's a godsend.'

'She did well, didn't she?' agreed Ruth without, however, answering the question. 'I told you you'd be OK,' she added to the newcomer.

Trish smiled but said nothing.

After the practice Lucy rushed straight

down to Sheena's flat. The light was on and the radio was blaring. She hammered on the door, but nobody answered. She continued to knock for many minutes, but to no avail. She tried to open the door, but it was locked. The radio played on. She could not force the door. She had no key.

She put her eye to the keyhole, hoping nobody would come onto the landing and catch her at it. But she could see nothing. She knocked once again, but without hope.

Frustrated, she turned away and went home.

Chapter 20

Lucy had a full morning of pupils on the Saturday. Had she known in advance about the need for someone to sort out Sheena, she might have cancelled them. But it was too late. She phoned Eileen early.

'Can you go down to Sheena's flat and see if she's all right? I couldn't get a reply last night.'

'It's a bit of a nuisance, Lucy.' Eileen was not exactly idle on a Saturday morning. 'Still, I've got some shopping to get down there. So I'll check up on her before I come home.'

'Can you make sure she gets to work? Saturday's their busiest day at the hair-dresser's and she might get the sack if she doesn't go in.'

So Eileen left her family to get their own breakfasts and was hammering on Sheena's door soon after eight o'clock. After a while she heard shuffling noises and the door opened a little. Sheena peered out to see who it was. She looked a real mess, pale and haggard, with ropey, unkempt hair.

'What do you want?'

'Lucy sent me. She was worried about you. You missed band last night. Can I come in?'

'Yeah,' she opened the door to let Eileen in, then pushed past her. 'Excuse me a minute.'

She rushed a few yards along the landing and pushed open the toilet door. Vomiting noises could be heard. Eileen walked further into the flat so that she did not have to listen to them. Except for the rumpled bed, which appeared to have been the scene of much activity, it was not too untidy, though no-body could say it was nicely decorated. Probably Sheena had as yet spent little time in it. In the tiny living area, out of sight of the bed, the baritone horn lay on the scruffy rug. A book of exercises stood open at page one on a music stand.

Perhaps Sheena was not beyond redemp-tion, after all.

When she returned Eileen made her force down some toast and coffee. In the wardrobe and chest of drawers she found some clean clothes for Sheena to put on and waited to make sure she did so. At eighteen she was still young enough to have good powers of recovery and within fifteen or twenty minutes was looking fit to walk the distance to the hairdresser's.

'So what kept you from such an important practice?' Eileen demanded, following her down the stairs.

'Sorry about that, Mrs Riley. I didn't mean to miss it. I just freaked out, I suppose.'

'Freaked out? What do you mean, freaked out?'

'I met this chap. He had this stuff. That's all.'

'What stuff? What chap?'

But Sheena felt she had already said too much.

'I go this way now, Mrs Riley,' she said as they emerged into the busy street. 'Tarra. Thanks for your trouble.'

'Wait a minute,' Eileen trotted after her. 'It's the festival this evening. You won't be meeting this chap again after work, will you? You won't be having any more stuff?'

'No fear. Another do like that'd finish me off.'

She hastened away. Eileen watched her departing figure, already recovered enough to walk with a swing. How long would she last? Would a girl like that ever see her fortieth birthday? Would she want to? Would anybody care if she did? It seemed such a shame.

Lucy fixed up for Alice and Gladys to pick up Sheena. She herself would be going to the Festival Hall early and coming back late. Harry's colliery band were competing in the top category, which was the last class to be held. Her own band, hurriedly named the Adlington Ladies for the entry form and the bank account, was in an earlier class. In fact, she saw when she arrived and was able to buy a programme, that they were first on. They were scheduled to play at 7.30 p.m. That was not good in a way. It left no room for latecomers. Also, in her experience, people who went on first seldom won a competition. At decision time they were never fresh in the adjudicator's mind. But it would please those like Ruth who had to hurry on to something else afterwards.

She and Harry were first there of their crowd. They lost no time in finding good seats and saving some for Eileen and Tom. Susie no doubt would want to be with the younger band members.

It was a large hall with row upon row of raked velvet-upholstered seating. Its glory days as an opera house had left it a legacy of ornamental plaster-moulded pillars and proscenium arch. There was an upstairs balcony and several boxes, now declared unsafe. Playing in that setting was going to be quite different from Rivington Church Hall. Better, she hoped. She had done everything she could and now it was up to the players themselves. So many things had gone wrong along the way that she found herself tense with the expectation of another piece of bad news.

But as time passed all seemed well. They sat and listened to the class for quartets and every time there was a gap between groups she looked around and found more of her flock had arrived. Eileen and Tom soon joined them, with Rachel and Rebecca Hetherington and Susie. Florrie and Wilfred had given Winifred a lift in, along with Mary, who had had to leave Les and William behind for once. Judith and Wendy were able to come on the bus, bringing Penny the horn player. Deirdre and Joan had got babysitters and brought their husbands with them on this special occasion. Doreen and Maureen were already there. They had already competed in the individual classes. Maureen had come second in her age group.

Time was passing. The adjudicator rose and delivered his assessment of the quartets. Where were the others?

It turned out they had been kept waiting

by the attendant who would not let them in until the speaker had finished. After he delivered his verdict and the winners were applauded, the door opened and dozens of people streamed into the auditorium, among them Alice and Gladys with Sheena, then Annette who had been brought along by Harold, of course. What a supportive husband he was, thought Lucy.

There was no sign of Ruth.

The interval came. Now they must go behind the curtains and set up their band. Lucy felt panic rising. If Ruth and Trish failed to turn up, they really would be sunk.

'If you see any sign of Ruth Anderton, send her round backstage at once,' Lucy begged Harry, as she and Eileen rose to go.

'There's plenty of time yet, love,' he reassured her. His mind was occupied with the chances of his own band.

She went the long way round, through the foyer, hoping to catch Ruth if she was just arriving. But saw no sign of her. She could not hang around. She had to do a headcount backstage and make sure that all the chairs and music stands were out ready. A tune-up would be a good idea, too. Of course, when she joined her musicians, everybody was waiting for her, including Ruth and Trish, who had gone straight back-stage, old hands at the game as they were, without bothering to venture out among the audience at all.

It was such a relief. Everybody was there, with her instrument and her music and nothing was missing. Lucy felt she had to sit down for a minute, just to let her heart stop pounding.

When the time came for the curtains to open they were all ready and seated and looked quite smart in black and white, though they were the only band to have no banners over their music stands. The adjudicator gave the signal and Lucy walked on, to general applause and bowed to the audience. There was some rather frenzied clapping and cheering from an elderly gentleman at the end of the third row. She did not recognise him.

'That's Eddie Pickerskill,' hissed Florrie, rather loudly. Lucy frowned at her, raised her arms, then pointed the baton at Mary for the solitary euphonium note which marked the opening of 'Prelude to a Storm'.

As soon as she heard it, she knew it was going to be all right. Her nerves vanished. The band made their entries, section by section, nice and cleanly. Everybody did as they should have. The tuning was good, the response to her crescendo and diminuendo gestures was perfect. She conducted as if in a dream. The sounds that came back at her were the ones she had despaired of ever evincing. Even the percussion was right. The final chord sounded and the audience broke into a spatter of applause before they remembered that there was more to come.

The 'Medley of Scottish Airs' was child's play after that. Both cadenzas were expertly dealt with and all the solo passages up to scratch. Annette did not fluff any notes on the cornet. This time the audience applauded wholeheartedly; Lucy bowed, put out a hand to her ladies, who rose and bowed, then the curtains closed and they had to move quickly to make way for the next competitors.

'Well done, everybody!' she whispered after their departing backs. Then she found Eileen and they grabbed a quick gin and orange before rejoining their husbands in the audience.

'I can't believe it's over!' gasped Lucy.

'It isn't,' Eileen reminded her.

Because they had been to the bar, they missed the band which followed them, but were back in the auditorium in time to hear the third entry, which was Great Hulme Motors. Glancing round, Lucy was pleased to see most of the others in the audience. Sheena, in particular, she must keep her eye on. Only Ruth Anderton was not there, with her drummer. Lucy had a suspicion about that Trish – there was something about the way she moved and the way she never spoke to anybody. But she did not dare voice it in case she was mistaken. It would be too embarrassing. Anyway, Ruth knew what was at stake. Like as not Trish was one of Ruth's kind, poor girl.

The curtains parted to reveal Great Hulme Motors in all their glory. Smart, tailor-made uniforms they all wore, red with gold trim. Every music stand sported red banners with the initials GHM wrought into a fancy gold monogram. The average age must have been well over forty.

When they started to play it was evident that their sound did not match their appearance for smartness. Somebody split a note. The basses were mistuned. A couple of middle entries were ragged and their pianissimos were not even throughout the band. However, they did have two baritones and two euphoniums, as well as three basses. Their Own Choice piece was simply a rousing march which gave everybody plenty of blowing, but the only scope for light and shade was to play the repeats more loudly the second time through.

'Don't worry love,' Harry told her. 'You were streets ahead of that lot.'

A couple more bands had their turn and then they came to the adjudication.

The adjudicator mounted the stage and began his assessment with the Adlington Ladies. Did that he mean had marked them bottom? Or was he taking them in the order in which they appeared?

It turned out he had placed them bottom, criticising their lack of proper uniforms and their failure to provide banners. Any band worth its salt took a pride in its appearance. Those who entered festivals must take them seriously and not demean themselves and the festival and brass playing in general with a slapdash approach. There was only one baritone, he added, and the instruments came nowhere near to matching, since some were brass and some were silver and appeared to be of different manufacture. He went on to say that although they had obviously put some work into the pieces, the overall sound was lacking in power. There simply was not enough beef for a brass band and not enough bass to balance with the cornets.

Lucy sat there stunned as the words floated across to her, not really believing what she heard. The only consolation was that Great Hulme Motors came second from the bottom.

As the adjudicator finished announcing his verdict and returned to the auditorium, accompanied by the sound of obligatory clapping, a figure at the end of the third row rose to his feet.

'Call yourself a judge?' shrieked Eddie Pickerskill. 'They'd get a fairer trial in Moscow!' He followed the adjudicator up the aisle, waving his fists and pouring out invective, until he was grabbed by two ushers and hauled out of the theatre.

'He's right,' said Harry. 'You were robbed.'

'But why?' Lucy wanted to know.

'I don't know,' Harry told her. 'Perhaps somebody slipped him a few quid.'

The Mackenzie Jaguar purred on into the night.

'I don't know much about brass,' said Harold, 'but I'm surprised you weren't placed higher.'

'I can't believe it,' Annette murmured, 'after all the trouble we took, all the attention to detail. Lucy left no stone unturned. We played like a dream. And all he did was criticise our appearance.'

That was a criticism to which Annette was utterly unaccustomed.

'I must say it didn't seem fair to me.'

'It was all such a waste of time. It's heart-breaking.'

'The audience liked you. You got more applause than those Motors.'

'Yes, but we were doing it to get a van for Mary. For the handicapped. That man who made such a fuss afterwards – you know – the one who had to be carried out. He promised Mary a van if we beat the Motors. We didn't have to win, just beat the Motors.'

'He promised Mary a van?' Harold almost

squeaked. 'He must be loaded.'

'Used to be a second-hand car dealer, I think.'

'Ah.' That explained it, as far as Harold was concerned. He swore as a pair of lights on full beam shone into his eyes. 'Perhaps he'll cough up, anyway, for a good performance.'

'Why should he? We didn't come up with our part of the bargain.'

'The Lions Club might get a van for Mary. Want me to ask them?'

'Oh would you?'

'It's just the sort of project they like. Not all of men are bastards, you know.'

'Why, darling, nobody ever suggested you were.'

There was a pause, then she spoiled it by adding: 'Well, not to my knowledge, anyway.'

Epilogue

It said a good deal for the dedication of the bandswomen that they all turned up to practice the following Wednesday – all except Joan and Deirdre. Not that anybody was whistling. There was no place for cheerful expectation any more. They had that rather grimly resigned but mutually supportive air of people who had just emerged from an air-raid shelter to discover in the cold light of dawn that their street had been devastated by a bomb. They made wry faces at one another and spoke in low voices. Chairs were set out by Alice and Gladys without a single word of dispute. One by one the members arrived, opened their cases, found their seats and blew into their instruments to warm them up.

Lucy surveyed the ranks, smiled at them, and was just opening her mouth to deliver a homily of reassurance, when there was the squeal of brakes outside as a car drew up. Its door was loudly slammed. The outside door was flung open and noisily shut again. Everybody turned to see who was guilty of such unseemly behaviour.

It was Florrie. She stood in the doorway, looking bigger than ever. Her face was flushed. There was fire in her eyes.

'Aye up, it's the Queen of the Night,' joked Gladys.

'That bloke!' bellowed her majesty.

'Which bloke, Florence?' Lucy wanted to know.

'Him as sat by the adjudicator.'

'The Officiating Officer?'

'Is that his title? I've got better names for him.'

'Well don't give them. Come and sit down. We're about to start.'

278

'What about him?' asked Eileen, who did want to know. Florence stood her case on end, put her elbow on it and panned the room dramatically.

'He was only a Director of Great Hulme Motors.'

'A director?'

'Aye a director. The boss, in other words, or one of them.'

'Not the adjudicator?'

That was Eileen, making sure she got it clear.

'No. Him as looked after the adjudicator. Gave him accommodation, drove him to and fro. You know, got him his tea and anything that took his fancy.'

'Surely that wouldn't make a difference?' Lucy protested. 'What could he do?'

'He could do a lot. And he did. As far as I can gather, he told him that we'd only entered for a bet.'

'Never!'

Gasps of disbelief.

'Wilf has a friend as plays for t'Motors. That's how I found out. It seems this chap said that we'd been boasting that we'd get the prize because we were better-looking than the men and all we had to do was show a bit of leg.'

'A bit of leg?' repeated Winifred in disbelief. 'A bit of varicose vein, in my case.'

But one or two of the others looked sideways at Annette.

'Did anybody here say that?' Lucy wanted to know.

There was silence. Their faces were blank and unmarked by guilt. Several 'not me's' and 'I never's' could be heard.

'Of course nobody said that,' Florrie went on. 'It was specially concocted just to put his back up; make him want to teach us a lesson.'

'And that's what he was trying to do,' said Lucy, folding her arms and nodding. Everything the man had said began to fall into place.

'Just teach us a lesson,' added Eileen.

'That must have been why he went on and on about what we looked like.'

'When he said we were demeaning ourselves and the festival.'

'That really hurt, that did.'

'What a rotten thing to do!'

'It's people who resort to underhand methods to swing things against their opponents that demean the festival.'

That, surprisingly, was Mary.

'Well said,' somebody felt it incumbent to add.

She spoke for them all. Their indignation knew no bounds. It was difficult to get them to pick up their instruments again and play. It was difficult to know what to give them to play. Suddenly there was nothing to play for.

Lucy rapped her conductor's stand to break up their little groups of mutual ire.

'Does everybody here want to continue with this band?' There was silence. 'Does anybody want to give up?' Again, silence. 'If anybody wants to leave, now is the time.'

Nobody left.

'All right, put up "Regimental Selection".'

Everybody groaned.

Trish was not at the practice, of course. Lucy sought out Ruth during the break.

'Any chance of Trish staying with us? She was so good.'

'She did well, didn't she? She's a cousin of mine. I sent out an SOS and she came running. All the way from Wolverhampton. She stayed over Saturday to hear the Stonemasons, then she had to go straight back on Sunday morning. I'm afraid you won't see her again.'

'What a shame,' said Lucy. 'Please tell her how grateful we are.'

'I'll certainly do that.'

'I'm sorry we had to have such a disappointing result, when we played so well.'

'Yes, it's tough, but no need to get upset.' Ruth's tone was bracing. 'Everybody who was there heard us. It was a specialised audience. Most of them knew one end of a euphonium from the other. In other words, he was not the only judge in the room. Do you know what I'm saying?'

'Yes. I think I know what you're saying. Thank you.'

Lucy felt slightly better after that. The subject of Trish was a sleeping dog she was prepared to let lie.

Eileen came to speak to her.

'Do you think we should buy some banners with the money we made at the carol concert?'

'There won't be enough left. I gave the vicar a donation. But it's not a bad idea to hold another one. Make some more money, pay off the interest-free loan for the bass, and then. I wish I'd thought to get some for the festival.'

'You have to order them a long time ahead.'

'And we didn't have a name to put on them until I entered us in December. I just thought up the Adlington Ladies on the spur of the moment.'

'We practise in Rivington now. So that name won't do any more.'

'We'll have to think of another one now.'

'Yes and this time we'll take suggestions. That'll help everyone to look forwards instead of backwards. Then we'll be prepared next time we hold an event.'

'Like another concert.'

'Of course.'

After the break she let the band members choose what to play, so they finished up with all the favourites from their small repertoire. They played 'Tightrope Walker' again. The Youth Club's drum kit was already set out, close to the piano and within range of her baton, so when the right time came, she hit the cymbal herself to crown Florrie's performance.

Afterwards Eileen helped stack away chairs as usual.

'That Trish,' she said to Lucy. 'Will we see her again?'

'I'm afraid not. She's Ruth's cousin, so she tells me. Lives in Wolverhampton'

'All that way?' Eileen stood holding a chair, hesitating, then, 'Do you know what I think?'

'Yes. But don't say it. We didn't beat the Motors. So no harm done.'

'I wondered if it might be – what they mean by a desperate remedy...'

'For a desperate situation. Quite.'

The system of giving lifts home to those who needed them was now routine. Eileen took Rachel and Rebecca, Florrie took Winifred, Lucy ferried Judith and Wendy. Rivington was no longer on their bus route.

Sheena sat in the back of the Hot Stompers' van as it clattered along under Gladys's guidance. She was very quiet.

Though she did not show it, she was hopping mad. A wrong had been done to them. She was tired of being on the losing side, of being numbered among the despised. Mrs Brindle and the band had been kind to her. They had deserved better.

She lit herself a fag.

'Don't go setting light to that newspaper in the back, there, will you!' called the ever-vigilant Gladys, eying her sternly in the rear-view mirror.

'Newspaper?' Sheena looked around, then realised she was sitting on a pile of old newspapers, neatly tied with box cord.

'Been there since Bonfire Night,' put in Alice. 'Time we got rid of them.'

'I'll take them off your hands, if you like,' Sheena offered. 'I've got a chest of drawers need lining.'

'Help yourself.'

'Drop me off at your house,' she called as they chugged down Babylon Lane. 'I'll walk the rest of the way.'

'Will you be all right? Do you want us to come with you?'

'It's only round the corner.'

They pulled up outside the Ainscough house and Sheena climbed out, picked up the baritone by its handle and put a sheaf of papers under one arm.

'Can I carry something for you?' asked Alice solicitously.

''S all right, thanks.'

Sheena clip-clopped off along the lamp-lit street, a small silhouette, laden on each side, but with a jaunty plume of smoke that coiled round behind her in the artificial light.

'Do you think she'll be all right?' mused Alice.

'She'll be just as all right as she wants to be, that one,' said Gladys.

Next morning Sheena brushed a pile of chopped hair along the tiled floor. It piled up on the brush as she went, like dead leaves on a roadman's brush, until it began to escape round the sides, leaving a clean strip the width of the brush head. Her anger and resentment had dissipated. She leaned on the brush handle and watched her boss clipping away at a customer's tresses – cutting away the untidy straggling strands and leaving order where chaos had been. She could do that.

Steve had got six years. He'd be out in three or four, if he could manage a bit of good behaviour. Time for her to learn the trade. She'd like cutting hair. You could have a good chat and earn well, especially if you could set up yourself. You could also save up and find a salon to rent. She could get a better flat. Somewhere for Steve to join her when he came out. They could be together.

That was worth working for.

'Don't stand there dreaming, Sheena.' Her employer's voice cut sharply into her reverie. 'Can you get Mrs Jones a coffee with two sugars? Then finish that floor. You've left a whole corner out over there.'

At lunchtime Lucy's telephone rang.

'Have you heard?' came Eileen's voice. 'Great Hulme Motors have lost their band room.'

'What happened?'

'It went up in smoke. Last night. In the early hours. They've lost all their music, apparently, and most of their percussion and some of their instruments are damaged beyond repair.'

'I suppose I should say I'm sorry to hear that, though it'd be hard to mean it. How did it happen?'

'I don't think they know yet. Stuart and Philip heard it from school. It seems the building was totally gutted. It was a wooden building.'

'Well keep me posted. Let me know if you hear any more. I just hope they don't think any of us was responsible.'

The publishers hope that this book has given you enjoyable reading. Large Print Books are especially designed to be as easy to see and hold as possible. If you wish a complete list of our books please ask at your local library or write directly to:

Dales Large Print Books
Magna House, Long Preston,
Skipton, North Yorkshire.
BD23 4ND

This Large Print Book, for people
who cannot read normal print,
is published under the auspices of

THE ULVERSCROFT FOUNDATION